MW01172935

JoMarie DeGioia

PUBLISHED BY:

Bailey Park Publishing

ISBN: 978-1-944181-42-0

The Daring Debutante

Book Three of the
Secret Hearts Series

by

JoMarie DeGioia

Chapter 1

London, England 1825

Brianna Ellsworth stood among the crowd at the first important party of the Season. She ran her gloved hands over the skirt of her new gown. It was in yet another pastel shade, this one violet. It was a bit more daring than the colors she had worn last year, but she was twenty years old now and it was time to get serious about finding a suitor and bringing him up to snuff. At least, that is what her good friend Patrice Prestwick's mother insisted upon all the time.

Brianna's aunt sat with several of the other older ladies in attendance, watching over the gathering with a practiced and discerning eye from her position at the other end of the ballroom. With Brianna's older sister Marianne happily settled these past two years now, and with a sweet baby girl to keep her and her husband occupied, Brianna only had Aunt Hattie to play chaperone. It was liberating, but also a touch frightening. How ever would Brianna know who was a worthy gentleman and who would play her false or attempt to hurt her?

"There are so many eligible gentlemen here this evening!" Patrice said. "I know my little sisters will take note of who was present and how many asked me to dance."

"I am glad I do not have such eager observers," Brianna said with a laugh.

"Yes. Polly and Paulette are sharp and have impeccable memories." Patrice lifted her glass of punch to her lips and smiled. "After last Season, I am at least relieved that our mother is less desperate."

Brianna nodded. "My sister told me some of it, Patrice. I am so glad all turned out well for Penelope."

"Penelope and Lord Devlin are so very happy," Patrice said. "And their little baby boy is so darling!"

Brianna smiled. "He is but two months older than my own niece. I am certain they shall grow to be great friends."

"Or my nephew will be as dashing as his father and leave broken hearts in his wake."

Brianna managed to smile but she would not say a word against Lord Devlin, Penelope's husband. She knew from her sister that he kept secrets close to protect just about everyone he cared about, and that he counted Marianne and Marcus among those treasured few. Still, she prayed that neither he nor anyone else ever learned of her secret. She had yet to unravel the truth of it herself.

"Let us worry over our own matches, Patrice," Brianna said with a laugh. "The Season has only just begun."

Patrice straightened and glanced over Brianna's shoulder. "And here comes the first intrepid suitors."

A sliver of hope broke through to Brianna as she turned to look at the group of gentlemen heading their way, though it was dashed most swiftly. Lord Wilbrey and Mr. Stilling seemed to be in the lead, with Lords Bottom and Erlington bringing up the rear. She mentally removed the latter two from her own consideration, having observed them over the past two Seasons. They seemed to give token attention to every young lady, for apparently neither of them was serious about taking a bride this or any year. Their formals strained across their midsections and their florid faces showed that they had indulged in more than the weak punch served at this function. To hear her brother-in-law speak of them, this was the usual condition of both gentlemen.

As for the other two, they seemed the more promising of the four prospects. Both were slender and elegant, Lord Wilbrey as fair as Mr. Stilling was dark. They had each paid their attention last Season, to both her and to Patrice among other young ladies. Neither had come up to snuff however, to the everlasting chagrin of both Mrs. Prestwick and Brianna's aunt. Brianna had her doubts that they would this Season either, but this was the way of the courtship dances was it not?

The four of them approached as if one man, and Brianna braced herself.

"Ladies!" Bottom gushed as they stood before her and Patrice. "You look lovely this evening."

"Yes, yes. Quite enchanting," Erlington said.

Wilbrey smiled winningly, his blue eyes sparkling. "Miss Brianna. Miss Patrice."

"Lord Wilbrey," they both answered.

"I would love to claim dances with each of you, ladies," he said, bowing his golden head. "Though I daresay I will not be able to decide which one of you will be the first."

"I believe I shall be the deciding factor, Wilbrey." Stilling dipped his head. "Ladies, I must claim a dance with each of you as well."

The gentleman's dark eyes darted between her and Patrice, a familiar glint in his gaze. He had courted her sister with much enthusiasm two years past and had even come close to claiming her hand in marriage. Brianna had serious doubts that a man could shift his affections so easily to another lady, let alone that lady's sister. Would she truly want one who could?

Bottom and Erlington talked among themselves, their eyes bright as they anticipated some sort of challenge between the two younger gentlemen.

"I say, Wilbrey." Bottom elbowed the blond gentleman. "Are you going to allow Stinky Stilling to take your prize?"

Brianna hid her smile at the nickname she often heard from her brother-in-law.

"Really, Stilling," Erlington laughed. "Wilbrey is stepping on your toes!"

Both Wilbrey and Stilling reddened, though Lord Wilbrey appeared to be embarrassed while Mr. Stilling's pique was more evident. However, neither appeared to be the sort to put down or pick up any challenge for either young lady, despite the other two gentlemen's enthusiastic encouragement.

His nose in the air, Stilling took Brianna's hand and brought it to his lips. He lightly buzzed against her skin. "I will return to claim our dance, Miss Brianna."

Wilbrey appeared affronted, but he soon recovered and bowed to both her and Patrice once more. "Until later?"

She and Patrice both nodded their heads and the gentleman hurried away from them. Bottom and Erlington stared after him and Mr. Stilling for a long moment, and then guffawed and slapped each other on the back.

"Ah, ladies," Bottom said with an easy bow. "I daresay we shall seek out your company later this evening."

"Yes," Erlington wiped his eyes. "If only to see those two fools stumble all over you both."

After they were in relative privacy, Patrice leaned closer. "Choose yours, Brianna," she whispered in her ear.

Dejected, she let out a sigh. "I fear none of these will ever do."

She stilled as she caught a glimpse of the dark-haired gentleman who had captivated her last year before his disappearance well before the end of the Season. She had hoped to see him this Season, but she never imagined that he would attend the very first party. Yet, there he stood at the refreshment table looking as though he wished to be just about anywhere else.

Patrice said something else about her sisters or her mother, Brianna was not certain which, but she barely heard her friend. No. With Lord Shaston in the room? She could pay attention to little else.

Oh, he looked as handsome as she remembered. And with his thick dark hair and smoothly chiseled jaw, not to mention how well he looked in his formals, she found him as compelling as he had been in her dreams these long months since his early departure last Season.

He had risen to his earldom two years past, according to the very well-informed Mrs. Prestwick, upon the sudden passing of his father. He was young for an earl, and apparently his estate and holdings called him from Town often. There was an air of mystery about him as well. If she had wanted to create the perfect gentleman to occupy her thoughts and attentions, she could not imagine one better suited to the task than Lord Shaston himself.

She pictured the arrangement of red roses she received two mornings past. There had been a card but no signature, which was passing strange. Was Lord Shaston her secret suitor? Perhaps he was the answer to the mystery, and would that not be a delightful discovery?

***

William Shaston, the Earl of Shaston, sipped from a glass of weak punch served at the party. He had managed to finish the bulk of his work at Shaston Court shortly after Easter and was now free to return to Town to circulate among the *ton*. No doubt his duties to estate and family would drag him back to Essex sooner rather than later, but he could surely use the diversions London amply provided at present.

The usual arrayment of ladies and gentlemen appeared to be in attendance this evening, and he looked about the gathering to see if any of his acquaintances were among the party guests. He had fled London before last Season had concluded, and he prayed that his past mistakes would neither be discovered nor spoken of in company this year.

"Shaston, you are back among the living!"

Will managed to refrain from wincing as Lord Bottom waddled over in his direction. His bosom chum,

Lord Erlington, accompanied him to no one's surprise.

"Bottom," he returned with a nod of his head. "Erlington. How does this evening find you?"

Bottom guffawed. "There is that blasted honorable address! See there, Erlington? I told you Shaston is still the ever-genial gentleman."

"Yes," Erlington laughed. "He is all cordiality."

Will blinked. "Whatever are you two clucking about?"

"We had heard you were to stay in the country when you left Society last Season, friend," Bottom said. "We speculated that you had developed country manners."

Will's lips thinned. "As you see, I did not remain. As to my manners, I am unaware of any fundamental change."

"More's the pity," Erlington grumbled. "Yet another chivalrous rival for the young ladies' affections. And it is rumored that you are quite the catch this Season."

Will did allow an eye roll at that. While it was true that his estate was quite profitable now, he doubted it would make him any more desirable than any other young gentleman this year.

"Do not tell me that you two are serious in your pursuits at long last," Will asked.

The other two men elbowed each other.

"Serious?" Bottom shook his head. "I do not know about that."

"Really, Shaston," Erlington added. "I fear you shall put a pall on the evening's fun."

"Fun?" Will asked.

"Yes, fun," Bottom said. "Flirting and dancing is fun, even though any spirits stronger than punch are nowhere to be had."

"Just so you do not give the young lady the impression that you mean more than a dance," Will said.

They gaped at him. "When did you become so stodgy?" Bottom asked.

Will blew out a breath. "I am not stodgy, I assure you. I simply do not wish to mislead any young lady regarding my intentions."

"Oh, intend to wed this Season, do you?" Erlington asked.

Will was not certain about that, but he wished to comport himself with more honor than he had last year. He would not share that with these two buffoons, however.

"I will not discuss this with you in company," he said with a scowl. "Surely after several Seasons you two would have developed more decorum."

Their mouths fell open for a moment, but they soon fell to laughing again.

Will set down his glass and turned from the two of them to cross the dance floor. A vision in violet caught his eye then, and recognition flicked over his nerves. Brianna Ellsworth. He only saw her profile, exquisite though it appeared even from this distance. Her honey-colored hair was upswept and coiled at her crown and her pretty gown showed as many of her assets as possible in company. How old was she now? Twenty, he believed.

She had appeared in his orbit over the last two Seasons, though they had never shared more than the occasional dance. He had first been enamored of her older sister, now the Countess of Lacey. He had been a foolish boy then, however. The time since, striving to make his father's legacy a success, had since hardened him as he struggled to grow into the very large space his father's sudden death had left in the earldom.

"Very pretty, is she not?" a female voice said close to his ear.

He stifled a cringe as he recognized that hateful lilt full of false congeniality. Shame crawled up his back and he clenched his fists.

"Lady Lasking," he said in a low voice, not bothering to even turn his head in her direction.

She laughed very softly. "Shaston, do you cut me so early in the Season?" she breathed.

He would not give the widow more than passing notice. Not after what she had done last year to nearly ruin his chances of ever being a man who would have made his father proud. He owned his part in his near-downfall, but the sin would not be repeated. He would die first.

Without another word for Elise Lasking, he made his way toward Miss Brianna. She turned as he approached, and he was snared by her big blue eyes. Her rosy lips parted, and he felt a smile stretch his own. She had grown more beautiful since he had seen her last, surpassing even the memories of her he had held close during his self-imposed seclusion in the country since leaving Town last Season.

"Miss Brianna." He sketched a pretty bow and

straightened. He noticed her companion then, one of the Prestwick young ladies. "Miss Prestwick."

"Patrice, Lord Shaston," the blond girl said. "Although you are forgiven any confusion among myself and my sisters."

Will grinned now. "Miss Patrice, yes."

"Do have pity on Lord Shaston," Brianna said, placing her gloved hand on his arm.

He glanced down at her delicate fingers, swallowing thickly. Her touch was light, innocent, but he felt her compassion as well.

"Pity, Miss Brianna?" he asked, patting her hand in turn. "Whatever for, pray?"

She tilted her head to the side, her eyes sparkling. "You have been gone from Town since last summer, my lord. You should be forgiven the trespass of forgetting our names upon meeting us again."

"I thank you for your kind pardon, Miss Brianna."

"He remembered your name," Patrice Prestwick said with a laugh.

Will dipped his head. "I do hope that my apparent misstep will not deter either of you from gracing me with dances this evening?"

"A dance would be lovely, Lord Shaston," Brianna said.

He boldly took her hand and brought it to his lips. "Would it be too forward to ask for that dance at present?"

Her companion's easy expression told him that the two young ladies were not rivals this Season. To his recollection, they had never been so. It was decidedly irregular, but perhaps it was because both of their elder sisters had married very well and there was less urgency on the part of their families to see the younger daughters so soon settled.

"That is," he continued nonetheless, "if Miss Patrice will allow your absence?"

"I shall persevere, Lord Shaston," the young lady said with a lift of her chin to a spot behind him.

He glanced over his shoulder to see his friend Evan Holbrook, Baron Wilbrey, making his hurried way in their direction. Looking back at Brianna, he gave her hand a gentle tug and she came to her feet in one graceful motion.

"Then let us commence," he said, turning to lead

her onto the dance floor.

They made their way through the steps of the dance, moving apart and coming back to each other as they traded places with the other dancers time and again. Every time he held her close to him, he could catch her scent. It was sweet and flowery and fresh. Her skin appeared flushed and her eyes bright as they moved faster still. Their steps were in sync, and she matched each of his perfectly.

"You are a wonderful dancer, my lord," she said breathlessly.

"My partner has much to do with it," he returned with a laugh. "I can almost believe no time at all has passed since last we danced together."

"And yet it has been nearly a year," she said as they twirled to a stop.

"That is far too long," he admitted. The number ended, and they clapped for the musicians. "Thank you, Miss Brianna."

"And I thank you, Lord Shaston."

He did not want their time together to end. This was passing strange, as he was accustomed to taking the pleasure of a dance and leaving to charm the next young lady. There had always been something about this particular lady, however. And had been so, ever since he first met her two years ago.

"What say you to a stroll out onto the terrace?" he asked.

She blinked in obvious surprise, and then smiled. "That sounds lovely."

He crooked his arm, and she tucked her hand into his elbow. As he escorted her through the throng, he caught sight of several partygoers taking note of his pointed attention. It was a simple stroll, but he suspected that the *ton* would read into it as they would.

They both walked to the railing and stood, looking out over the gardens. The gardens were arranged much like any of those in Town, in his experience. Lit with pretty lanterns and lined with paths meant for clandestine entanglements. He would not attempt so with her, though. She deserved more respect than that. There was danger there as well. Were he to get her alone in the darkened garden he might be unable to resist the lure of her close company.

"How did you occupy yourself since last summer,

my lord?"

He shrugged. "I had my father's estate to tend to, Miss Brianna."

"You mean to say your estate, do you not?"

The echo of pain struck him anew. "I suppose I do."

She nodded. "I know some of what that work involves. My brother-in-law is often occupied with business."

"Yet he and your sister have welcomed a little one just this year."

Her face lit with joy. "Yes, little Hannah is simply beautiful!"

"I trust she is adored by her favorite aunt?"

She gave a musical laugh and tapped his arm. "Oh, yes." Her gaze grew shuttered. "Though I believe they are wishing for more privacy now that they are a family."

"What do you mean? Lacey's house, and his other holdings, are quite large are they not?"

"They are, yes. Still, it has been nearly two years now."

"Feeling a bit crowded, are you?"

"No, not me." Her lips turned down in a pout that appeared wholly unpracticed. "I simply do not wish to become a burden."

A burden. As he had felt shouldering his responsibilities to the estate for these past two years.

He took her hand as he had before. "You can never be a burden, Miss Brianna." He brought his brow to hers, so close they were nearly touching. "You are a treasure."

Her eyes widened and after a quick glance about the space he saw that they were nearly alone. Brushing her lips with his, he felt his pulse quicken. Stunned, he began to draw away when she leaned up on her toes to press her mouth to his.

Chapter 2

Brianna gasped as her lips lingered on Lord Shaston's. Her body tingled and she longed for him to deepen the kiss. When she opened her mouth to him, he suddenly straightened and put some space between them. It was mere inches truly, but to Brianna he felt as far away as if he were clear across the terrace. His face reddened and his captivating blue eyes opened wide. His well-formed mouth dropped open before he closed it with a snap.

"Forgive me," he murmured.

She mumbled something in response, but she did not want to forgive any blessed thing. His lips had been so soft on hers, and then insistent as she had returned his caress.

"I have monopolized your company for too long," he rushed out. "Allow me to escort you back to your companion."

She nodded mutely and placed her hand in the crook of his offered elbow. She could still smell his fresh and spicy scent and she was suddenly seized with the longing for him to hold her in his arms.

Patrice's brows rose as they neared her, but Brianna could think of nothing to explain their quick return.

"Miss Brianna, thank you again," he said with a bow.

He nodded in Patrice Prestwick's direction and swiftly disappeared into the crush of partygoers.

"That was abrupt," Patrice said.

"Yes." Brianna attempted to locate him in the ballroom, following every dark-haired gentleman with her eyes. "It appears so."

"Lord Shaston is so charming and gregarious. Though he is usually far more attentive, if I recall correctly."

"He was, Patrice. Ever so much." She could not see hide nor hair of him at the moment, however. "Until he was not."

"Passing strange," her friend said. "Whatever transpired on the terrace?"

Brianna's head snapped back as she looked at Patrice. "You saw us on the terrace?"

"No, but I did see the two of you come from that direction."

Relief nearly swamped her. "We were on the terrace, yes. Nothing transpired, however."

"Nothing?" Patrice crossed her arms. "I have never known you to dissemble, dear friend."

Brianna found a smile, feeling her own cheeks heat now. "I am not. Nothing untoward occurred." *Except for that kiss.* "Nothing at all."

Patrice eyed her again, but Brianna was saved from making some sort of excuse when one of her friend's younger sisters called her over. The girl appeared to be quaking in her slippers.

"What has Polly overheard now?" Patrice wondered aloud. "I am certain nothing happens that she or Paulette do not learn of within moments."

Had the girl seen her and Lord Shaston on the terrace? No, Patrice's little sisters were clear across the ballroom. She gave a silent prayer of thanks.

"Go," Brianna laughed. "Before the girl explodes."

Patrice nodded with a smile and left Brianna on her own. She caught sight of Mr. Stilling headed in her direction, so she turned and hurriedly made her way over to where her aunt was sitting.

"Brianna, dear!" Aunt Hattie smiled sweetly at her. "You remember Mrs. Brooks and Mrs. Harding."

Brianna nodded to her aunt's companions. "Yes, ladies. Very nice to see you both."

"And you, Miss Brianna," Mrs. Brooks said. "I say, you look absolutely lovely this evening."

"She always does," Mrs. Harding added with a smile.

Brianna dipped a curtsey in response to the compliments.

"Are you having a good time, dear?" her aunt asked.

"Yes, Aunt." She pressed a finger to her temple. "But I fear I have a bit of a headache."

"Oh no." Aunt Hattie came to her feet. "Let us call for the carriage."

Brianna struggled not to let her relief show as she took her aunt's arm. Several guests present took pointed notice of them as they passed toward their host and hostess. They politely gave their regards before calling for the carriage. Soon they were settled inside for the short ride to Marianne and Marcus's townhouse.

"A headache is nothing to ignore, dear. It is far too early in the Season to wear yourself out."

"Yes, Aunt."

"I hope that you did not overdo it on the dance

floor."

"Hardly, Aunt. I only danced once."

She appeared thoughtful. "True. Was Lord Shaston too much for you to bear?"

Brianna's cheeks flamed anew, and she vehemently shook her head.

"No, Aunt."

"Well, when we get back you must go straight to bed. Truly, you are quite flushed."

"Yes, Aunt."

Shame bit at her as she continued to mislead her sweet aunt. She could not face the crowd at the party had she stayed, though. However, when they arrived at the townhouse, there were apparently more people disappointed than her aunt.

"Are you back already?" her sister Marianne called as they passed the doorway to the front parlor.

"Your sister was not feeling well," Aunt Hattie answered.

Marianne came to the entry, worry etched on her face. Some of her thick blond hair was pulled back to her crown and the rest left to float about her shoulders. There were faint shadows beneath her eyes, however. Brianna knew that the baby tended to fuss during the night and her sister and Marcus were loath to leave her in the nurse's care. Little Hannah must be sleeping at present, however. Brianna felt even more guilty for feigning any illness.

"Just a bit of a headache," Brianna said with a small smile.

"Oh, Bree. Thank goodness."

"Did you enjoy the party?" Marcus asked as he crossed to join her sister.

Brianna inclined her head. "I did. It was quite a crush, however."

"It certainly was," their aunt agreed.

Marianne and Marcus shared a warm look and he smiled at Brianna. "I am not surprised, given it was the first party of the Season."

"The first *important* party of the Season, husband," her sister said with a nod.

"Important?" Marcus rolled his eyes. "If you insist."

Marianne clicked her tongue. "Bree, go on upstairs right away. Sleep should make your head feel much better."

"Thank you, I shall."

They turned from her and returned to the parlor where they had no doubt been cuddling together in temporary peace before the baby made her presence known once again.

"I think I am for my bed as well," Aunt Hattie said. "I admit I am relieved to be home early this evening."

Brianna just nodded and bade Marianne and Marcus good night before following their aunt upstairs. Aunt Hattie turned down the hall toward her room and Brianna made for her own. The Earl of Lacey's townhouse was very large, and Marcus had been quite generous with her and Aunt Hattie after he married Marianne. They had trod a tumultuous path to get to their happy life, and Brianna could only hope that she would be half as fortunate in her choice of a life mate as they both were.

Her own room rivaled Marcus and Marianne's in luxury and comfort. She had a large bed draped with rose and gold fabrics and there was a very comfortable armchair set near the gilded fireplace. The space was very pretty and moving into it had thrilled her to her toes after what they had all gone through.

Coming to London two years ago with very little in their

coffers had been arduous. Marianne had set herself on a dangerous path for Brianna and their aunt's sakes before Marcus and she fell in love, and now Brianna believed that they deserved to live in privacy with their new little daughter.

Her maid arrived to assist her out of her pretty purple gown and into her nightgown and, once she was alone again, she stretched out on the fine, plump coverlet and let her eyes drift closed. Now at long last she could relive the delicious sensation of Lord Shaston's lips on hers. For those all-too-brief moments, it had seemed like they were the only two people at that crowded party. She had longed for their embrace to deepen, to go on for even longer than the length of their dance. When he had stepped away, however? Even that memory faded now.

She was once again wrapped in loneliness in her pretty, borrowed bedchamber.

***

Will sat alone in the crowded pub. He was in no mood for company. Even though Lord Wilbrey had offered to accompany him when he had informed him of his escape, he truly had not wanted to discuss the virtues of the young ladies present at the latest round of parties. Instead, he sought solace and tried his level best to blend in with the rabble.

Those present ranged from workmen to gentry. Some were loud and boisterous, and others were quiet and sullen as he himself was. Escape had been essential, after taking advantage of Brianna Ellsworth's innocence out there on that terrace. Ah, but the taste of her...

"What can I interest you in, milord?" one of the serving girls asked.

He eyed her assets, shown to plump advantage in her simple dress, and shook his head.

"Just an ale, please."

"Ooh, you got a nice way of asking!" She winked. "Maybe you would like to go upstairs in a bit?"

Will shook his head again. "The ale will do, thank you."

A dark-haired gentleman perhaps roughly thirty years old leaned over from the next table. "You could have had that one for nearly nothing. Bet she would've let you do whatever you like."

Will glared at him. "She might be a serving girl, but she deserves some respect."

The other man sneered and his brown eyes narrowed. "Don't like you telling me what I should do, all high and mighty."

Will's hands clenched and he itched to punch him in his leering face. Taking a breath, he made the decision to put the man from his notice. The girl brought him his ale and lingered for a few moments before leaving to tend to the other patrons. As he drank, he thought back to what had happened, or had nearly happened, at the party.

He had not meant to touch Brianna Ellsworth. Not outside of a kiss to her hand or a turn on the dance floor. But seeing her again after nearly a year, dancing with her again, he could almost forget what a weak-willed fool he had been last Season. Seeing Elise Lasking had brought it rushing back with sickening clarity. Brianna had been a breath of fresh, sweet air and he could do nothing but breathe her in deeply.

She had appeared so upset and downcast out there on the balcony. He should not have touched her and, once he had, he'd longed to pull her close. Putting his lips on hers had been madness, but nothing compared to the desire that had struck him when she had initiated another kiss and silently beseeched him to deepen it. Her daring reaction had fueled his passions and his protectiveness. She had worn her confusion on her beautiful face, but he had been unable to give her a reason that would make any sort of sense. He'd known full well why he'd been drawn to kiss her, but no notion why he'd been compelled to withdraw with such haste.

Out of the corner of his eye, he saw the crass gentleman grab the serving girl's arm in what appeared to be an unwelcome touch. When she slapped him, he seemed almost shocked that she should rebuff him. Will raised a hand to the pub owner, who he believed to be a good sort of gentleman. The big man took a look at the frightened serving girl and strode over to the table.

"See here, I don't allow any such behavior in my establishment."

The man came to his feet. "Do you know who I am?" he sputtered. "I may not have a title, but I am a man of consequence!"

He caught Will's eye as he squared his shoulders. "I saw you mix in my business, my lord."

Will schooled his expression.

"He be an earl and very welcome here, which I can't say for you." The pub owner began to forcibly remove the miscreant. "Now out with you!"

"I'll go, I'll go." The man glared at Will. "Mark my words, my lord. I shall prove of more consequence than the lot of you earls and such. Believe it."

It was a strange manner of threat, but Will simply gazed back at him. With another scathing look in Will's direction, the man finally left.

Will finished his ale and waved away the offer of another one before taking his own leave. He gave no further thought to the distasteful pub patron and, as he settled against the squabs, he braced himself for a long, lonely night with no one but himself for company.

Why had he returned to Town? He supposed he could no longer hide out in the country now that the Season had once again commenced. There would soon be rides in the park and making calls. Sending flowers and notes of thanks and dancing attendance on members of the *ton.* It was all part of the courting ritual, as it had been for generations. He did not require a wife in any hurry, but he longed to have someone in his life whose sweetness could wash away the sour taste left from his mistakes of last Season. Again, he thought about those blissful moments he had held Miss Brianna Ellsworth in his arms.

His mother continued in good health though her sadness since his father's passing cast a pall over the house in Essex. Even his usually cheerful little sister Violet seemed to fade in the atmosphere. The man's death had caught them unawares but at least Will had been able to steer the ship, so to speak, afterwards. Their marriage had been a very happy one, which no doubt led to his mother's demeanor now. Will hoped to emulate their life together whenever he ultimately chose a bride. He had flirted and danced with several ladies over his years in Society, but he feared that his misstep of last Season would doom any chance he had at future happiness. He did not put it past Lady Lasking to tell all and sundry what had happened. He had been lonely, he supposed. And foolish.

He arrived at his townhouse in Mayfair and absently checked the salver for any missives or cards that had arrived since he had left earlier in the evening. An envelope was sitting waiting, his name written in a familiar spidery handwriting. The hairs on the back of his neck rose.

"Bloody Elise," he grumbled.

He took a breath and tore open the envelope. As she had tonight at the party, Lady Lasking attempted to exert control over him. In the note she requested a renewal of their liaison.

"Not in a million years," he spat.

He tore the note in pieces and handed them to his butler, Carson.

"Dispose of these, please."

The older man nodded his head. "Certainly."

Will turned to go up to his room but stopped. "Please let me know if I receive any other communication from Lady Elise Lasking."

"Yes, my lord."

Will thanked him and continued up the staircase. He should refuse to accept any correspondence from her but he felt it would be better to simply not acknowledge receipt. It was a small thing, declining to respond to that bitch in even this small way, but it brought him some comfort. He had to hold on to his convictions. He would not become the weak-willed man he was last summer.

His valet Cates helped him out of his finery, and he was soon settled into his bed. The chamber was spacious and the bed very large. At least last year's memories did not taint this room. He had never had a lady of any sort here, despite Lady Lasking's manipulations. It was cold comfort, but he would take it as it was.

On the morrow he would seek out Miss Brianna. He would see flowers sent in the morning, and perhaps pay a call at the Earl of Lacey's townhouse as well. The past two Seasons he had flirted with and danced with several young ladies, but none had filled his mind like she did.

When he had retreated to the country in the middle of the Season, he had feared that he would return to find her married. She was still unencumbered but how long would that condition persist? She was sweet and beautiful with a streak of determination he had never suspected. Her depth of feeling and devotion to her sister was commendable as well. The combination was intoxicating.

He would not squander the chance to find happiness, no matter how clumsily he sought it. If he were ever so fortunate as to get her in his arms again? He feared he would never be able to let her go.

Chapter 3

Brianna awoke to the smell of chocolate and stretched with a smile. Her maid bustled about the room as Brianna sat up.

"That smells heavenly, Suzie!"

The maid laughed. "The countess said those very words."

Brianna smiled. "I do think her ladyship and I are very often of one mind."

Suzie nodded. "Will you be riding in the park this morning, miss?"

Brianna thought for a moment. Oh, would Lord Shaston be there?

"I believe so, Suzie." She glanced toward the windows, seeing the light peeping between the drawn draperies. "No doubt it will be a lovely day for a ride."

She was less sure of precisely who she would be riding with in the carriage. No doubt Marianne was still tired, her hot chocolate indulgence aside. Aunt Hattie was the next best companion, but the woman was not very enamored of riding in the open air through the throngs at the park. Brianna loved it, however. To see and be seen, to connect and converse with any number of ladies and gentlemen in the beautiful spring air.

Suzie dressed her in a lovely pink day dress sprigged with small flowers and swept her light brown hair into braids coiled at her crown.

"Will this suit, miss?"

Brianna regarded her reflection in the glass as she sat at the vanity. "Very well, yes. No doubt the spring sunshine calls for a deep bonnet this morning."

"I shall have your bonnet and gloves ready in the hall, miss."

"Thank you, Suzie."

The maid curtseyed and left. Brianna stood once more and ran her hands over her pretty dress. The earl took prodigious care of her, truly treating her like the sister he never had. She was blessed to live with them both here and in the country, but her new Season's wardrobe only made her wish to be less of a burden. Resigned to another day of this static existence, she put on a smile and went belowstairs to join her family in the breakfast room.

She found her sister and aunt within.

"Good morning!" she sang, crossing to the sideboard to

serve herself breakfast.

"Good morning, dear," her aunt said.

Aunt Hattie looked lovely this morning. She wore her years very well and was still as pretty as their mother had been. "I take it you are no longer plagued by last night's headache?"

Brianna shook her head as she joined them at the table. "Not at all, thank you. A good night's rest was just the thing."

"Hmm," her sister intoned.

Marianne's eyes narrowed and her lips quirked, as if she did not quite believe Brianna's headache tale. It would not be the first time an Ellsworth woman had used such an excuse, as Marianne had made use of it quite a bit during their first Season in Town. Of course, Brianna knew now that she had been meeting Marcus in secret. If only Brianna had such a delicious secret to conceal instead of embarrassment from pressing her interest toward Lord Shaston.

Brianna's cheeks heated but she focused on the plate in front of her.

"There are a large number of floral arrangements

in the entry," the earl said as he joined them. "I take it they are for our sister?"

Marianne chuckled. "Who else?"

The earl bent to kiss his wife's offered cheek and straightened. "I caught your meaning, love. I shall rectify my error."

Marianne waved a hand. "I am not feeling the least bit neglected, Marcus."

Brianna took in the picture her sister and the earl made, once more filled with happiness for their situation. She had to find her own way, however. That was never clearer to her than this morning. She came to her feet in a rush.

"Bree, what is your hurry?" Marianne asked her.

"You barely touched your breakfast," Aunt Hattie added.

"I had chocolate in my room," Brianna said.

Marianne and their aunt shared a look before her sister grinned.

"I daresay Bree is in a hurry to see the flowers," she said.

Brianna took a breath and bobbed her head. "As you say."

Without another word, she left the room, bound for the

front entry. She came to a stop as she saw the array of blooms filling the space. The earl had not exaggerated. There were no less than five arrangements awaiting her. Would she find the red roses this morning?

"These cannot possibly be just for me."

Marianne would not receive flowers, though. Not from any suitor, that was. Marcus was fiercely protective and would call a man out if he dared to show attention in his wife's direction. His chivalry had served them all well in keeping Marianne's secret safe.

Still, Brianna checked the calling cards accompanying the flowers, starting with one arrangement of lovely yellow roses.

"Lord Wilbrey," she murmured.

The card only bore his name and title. It was not surprising that the blond gentleman sent such addresses. It seemed that she had received them from him nearly every day last Season, and it appeared that the tradition would continue. He seemed to pay addresses to several young ladies, and she pondered that his floral bill must be quite high.

The next drew her, a pretty arrangement of white

roses and deep blue irises. The card was from Lord Shaston and her heart gave a thump.

"I enjoyed our encounter last evening, and hope that you are doing well today," she read aloud. "I look forward to sharing your company again very soon."

Encounter? Oh, what a loaded word. Of course, only the two of them would truly know what had happened out on the terrace last evening. Still, the memory caused her to flush anew.

"Are those from a gentleman you favor?" Aunt Hattie asked as she joined her.

"What?" Brianna held the card close. "Um, yes. Lord Shaston."

"The newest earl, yes."

Brianna nodded. "You saw us dance together last evening, Aunt."

"That I did. And a beautiful pair you made."

She quirked a brow at her aunt. "Pray do not order wedding flowers just yet."

Aunt Hattie waved a hand. "I am not pressing you to marry, dear. I just want you to be as happy as Marianne."

"I have little hope to claim that much happiness," she

said with a laugh.

Her aunt smiled. "Still, this attention bodes well for the Season."

Brianna held on to the card as she crossed to the other arrangements. "Lord Wilbrey sent the yellow roses."

"A fine gentleman."

She looked over the others, reading their cards aloud. None of these held a note as Lord Shaston's had, just their names.

"Mr. Stilling."

"Lord Bottom?" her aunt asked.

"Yes, though I cannot imagine why. Both he and Lord Erlington do not appear to seriously court anyone this or any Season."

A glimpse of red caught her eye, and she froze. This fifth arrangement was smaller than the others and had first been hidden behind Lord Wilbrey's. Though small, it held six sumptuous deep red roses.

"He did send them," she murmured. She bent her head to the blooms and breathed in. Their scent was almost too rich, and a shiver went through her.

"My, those are beautiful," her aunt said.

Brianna stroked one of the silky petals as she searched for a card. She found it addressed to her and turned it over.

"Who sent them?" Aunt Hattie asked.

Brianna turned the card over again. "There is no signature."

"That is strange."

Brianna nibbled her bottom lip before holding the card out to her aunt. "Not really. This is not the first such arrangement I have received."

"What?" Her aunt plucked the card from Brianna's fingers and scowled. "How many?"

"This makes two since we came back to Town."

"This is beyond peculiar."

"What is?" Marianne said as she joined them.

"Brianna has been receiving flowers from a gentleman who does not sign his name."

Marianne's brows rose and then she grinned. "Perhaps one of them in particular wishes to attract your interest above the others?"

"Why would a gentleman send two arrangements?" Aunt Hattie asked.

"To be certain that you are thinking of him, Bree."

"Without signing his name to the second?" Brianna asked.

Marianne shrugged. "They are quite beautiful. And have you not spent some time puzzling over this suitor's identity for the past three days?"

"I suppose."

Could Lord Shaston have sent two arrangements, the beautiful irises and these sinful red roses? Her heart gave that thump again.

"Perhaps she can guess who the gentleman is," Marianne said.

"What?" Brianna flushed. "No, I have no notion."

"Then perhaps you can drop hints when you speak to the gentlemen in the park this morning," Aunt Hattie said.

Marianne clasped her hands together. "Yes! Let me tell Marcus that I will join you this morning."

Brianna smiled. "Truly?"

Marianne nodded. "I suppose I can bear to be away from our little love for a couple of hours."

Brianna raised her brows. "Can you?"

"I will just look in on her now. It will not take but a moment."

She flew up the stairs and Brianna and her aunt laughed together.

"I suppose I should get my gloves and bonnet."

"And I will call for the carriage," Aunt Hattie said.

***

Will let out a breath as he sat on his horse, eager for the crush to move on the preferred track of the park. His horse was apparently of a like mind, for he snorted and tossed his head impatiently.

"Easy," he said, patting the animal's neck.

At least it was a nice morning. He had decided to jump into this Season with both feet after all, and this was part of the required activities. There were open carriages lining the track, and other gentlemen like him jockeying for position as they sought to see and be seen. His heart gave a thump as he spied a certain young lady just a few carriages from where he stood. She sat with her sister, the Countess of Lacey. As he managed to move closer, Miss Brianna tilted her head back for a moment and the sunlight limned her perfect visage.

"Is this not lovely?" he heard her exclaim.

"Yes very," the countess replied, "but do not let the sun hit those smooth cheeks, Bree. Aunt Hattie will be very upset with me if I allowed you to freckle."

Brianna laughed, a musical sound that wrapped around him. He pulled alongside their carriage and called out a greeting.

"Good morning, Lord Shaston," the countess said. "Look, Bree. It is Lord Shaston."

"As you see." Will dipped his head and faced Brianna. "May I say that the two of you make a very pretty picture this morning."

Brianna beamed a smile, her face alight with pleasure. Was it due to his arrival? He could perhaps flatter himself that it was so.

"It has been too long since my sister and I rode together like this," she said.

"Truly?" he asked.

"Yes, and we have missed it," the countess said.

"You, Lady Lacey, have a very good reason to miss such activities, I believe," he said.

"Indeed, and the earl and I appreciated your gift and your congratulations."

"My pleasure." Will nodded. "It seems that motherhood becomes you."

The countess waved a hand in dismissal, but Brianna took hold of it in her own. "There is not a more deserving woman than my dear sister."

"I pray that you will be as fortunate someday, Bree."

Brianna's face wore her doubt as her fair brows drew together. Did she truly doubt she would ever be as lucky as her sister?

"Perhaps Lord Shaston has an opinion?" the countess teased.

The two of them fell to laughing again but soon schooled their expressions to affect the proper genteel countenance one expected to find on young ladies riding in an open carriage through the park. The effect was charming, and he winked at the younger sister.

"Miss Brianna, you surely have a veritable crush of suitors this Season."

Her smooth cheeks turned pink. "I do not know about a crush."

"She does, Lord Shaston. In fact, we were just attempting to puzzle out the identity of one of them."

"Truly?"

"He is not an admirer, exactly," Brianna protested.

"Is he not? Did he not send a most romantic arrangement of flowers?"

"He did."

Will hid his smile. Was she speaking of the irises he had sent to her? They were a very pretty flower, nearly as pretty as Miss Brianna herself, but he had never heard them declared particularly romantic.

The countess pursed her lips as she apparently thought the matter through. "I will tell you. Why do we not hint about the flowers with the gentlemen we meet this morning?"

Brianna shook her head. "Oh, no! I do not want to seem ungrateful."

"Really, Bree. You have every right to know who is sending such things. What do you say, Lord Shaston?"

Will was quite confused. "I take it these particular flowers were sent anonymously?"

The countess blinked and then grinned at him. "Indeed, they were. It is most captivating, which I suspect may be the gentleman's intention?"

He puzzled over the matter for a moment. What sort of man would do such a thing? To present a mystery for the express purpose of piquing a young lady's interest? When he looked back at the two women, he found them both regarding him with acute interest.

"I will leave you ladies to your mystery, then." He smiled and dipped his head. "Miss Brianna, may I expect the pleasure of your hand in a dance this evening?"

Her eyes sparkled. "Oh yes, Lord Shaston."

"I shall bid you farewell until then." He nodded to the countess. "May you both enjoy your morning."

Out of the corner of his eye he saw the distasteful man from the pub last evening. As Will watched, the gentleman seemed to catch sight of something, or someone, and turned his mount as best he could to hurry in the other direction. Will thought for a moment to follow him. He appeared almost furtive. Had the man seen him and feared Will would force a confrontation?

Lord Wilbrey arrived on horseback just then and Will was forced to keep his place while his friend charmed both Brianna and her sister. Evan was all smiles and genteel manner, as he usually was. Will made a mental note to chide him about it later at the club.

"I say, the two of you are quite possibly the prettiest ladies in the park this morning," Evan said.

Brianna and the countess appeared to take his friend's comments in stride and in the ease in which he no doubt meant them. They spoke of the mysterious flowers again, but nothing on Evan's face indicated that he was Brianna's mystery suitor. As they conversed, Will watched the younger woman, and he did not see any partiality on her part toward his friend, either. Good. At least Will would not have to call him out. He smiled inwardly at the direction of his thoughts.

The two of them soon bade farewell to Brianna and the countess and rode through the park together.

"I believe I shall call an early end to my promenade this morning."

His friend's brows rose but he shrugged. "Something troubling you, Will?"

It was his turn to shrug. "Perhaps."

"I shall catch up with you later on, then."

Will rode on home and read through some papers that had been awaiting his attention. As the hour grew later, he made the snap decision to avoid the parties this evening. As much as he longed to dance with Brianna, he had no desire to see Lady Lasking.

After dining alone, he changed to head out to his gentlemen's club. He sat alone at a table, slowly letting himself get deep in his cups as his mind worked on the puzzle of Miss Brianna Ellsworth and her veritable legion of suitors. Aside from Lord Wilbrey and Stilling, the girl was attracting enough attention that she was receiving flowers from multiple gentlemen. Who, pray, sent her anonymous tokens of affection? As he ran through the litany of gentlemen who might be the culprit, Wilbrey entered the club.

"Shaston!" Wilbrey lifted his hand as he approached. "I see you were of like mind."

"Hello, Evan."

His friend sat and waved at a server to order a brandy for himself. "You appear to be working out a dilemma."

"Evan, who would send flowers anonymously to a young lady?"

"Are you speaking in general or particularly of the Ellsworth chit?"

Will nodded. "Miss Brianna, yes."

"Hmm." Evan lifted his glass in a silent salute. "Just this evening she was asking about red roses."

"You saw her, then?"

Evan grinned. "Danced with her, too."

Will said nothing to that. "So, the unclaimed red roses?"

"Neither Bottom nor Erlington possess the finesse or aplomb to be anything approaching subtle," Evan said.

Will smiled. "Agreed. Stinky Stilling, then?"

"I am quite certain he sent her flowers, but he would never take the risk of not signing his name."

"No, he would want the credit to be sure."

"Did you send her flowers?"

Will arched a brow.

"Of course you did." Realization dawned on Evan's face. "Oh! It is like that, is it?

The back of Will's neck grew hot. "I do not catch your meaning."

Evan laughed. "You prefer the Ellsworth chit, Will. Why dissemble?"

Will looked about the club and saw that most of

the others present were older gentlemen with no apparent care about their set. No doubt the young bucks were making the rounds of the parties still.

"All right, yes. But do keep your voice down."

"Are you at last going to settle down in marital bliss?"

"I am not at all certain that I deserve her."

Evan snorted. "You are wealthy. Well-regarded. Young and, if the approving glances from the women present at any number of parties, you are passably handsome."

Will chuckled. "As you say."

"Then what can be the issue? Can this have anything to do with whatever happened last Season?"

Will's lips thinned. He had shared none of what had happened last summer, not even with his closest friend. Shame swirled in his belly.

"Yes," was all he would say.

Evan's brow furrowed. "What the devil happened last year?" he asked softly.

"I cannot speak of it."

Evan wore an expression of confusion on his face, but Will knew he would not pry any deeper. He looked about and came to his feet. "This club is dreadfully dull this evening.

Join me at the pubs?"

Will shook his head. "I do not think so, friend."

Lord Wilbrey took his leave and Will departed for his townhouse. His butler took his hat and lifted his chin in the direction of the salver.

"You have a few messages, my lord. One from Lady Lasking, I am afraid."

Will sifted through a few letters and found hers. Like the previous, she spoke of renewing their liaison. "Please dispose of this, Carson."

"Yes, my lord."

He went into his study and sat beside the cold hearth. Would he ever be free of the disgust the mere thought of last summer elicited?

Carson popped into the study sometime later, an expression of worry on his face.

"Do you need anything else, my lord?"

Will glanced at the clock on the mantle and saw it was nearly one o'clock.

"No, Carson. Please find your bed, and let the others know I need nothing more this evening."

The butler appeared to wish to say something, but

Will knew he would ultimately heed his words. He had followed Will from the country to Town and was fiercely dedicated to him. He had been his father's man, and Will felt fortunate to have him.

"Very good, my lord."

Will still brooded, but just a few minutes later he heard a soft knock at the front door. He rose and went into the entry, not wanting the staff to worry about a late-night visitor. It was most likely Lord Wilbrey, wanting to pick up their conversation at the club.

"That is not going to happen," he grumbled.

He pulled open the front door to find Miss Brianna Ellsworth standing there, still clad in her evening gown.

"What…? Miss Brianna?"

She appeared nervous but then she sent him a look from the corner of her eye. "I know your secret."

He felt a wave of nausea crash over him.

"No," he breathed.

Chapter 4

Brianna watched as Lord Shaston's face turned white.

"Oh, my!" She rushed in and shut the door behind her. "Let us go into this room and sit down. Upon my word, you look very ill."

He blinked at her and gave a shaky nod. "All right."

She gripped his arm and urged him into the front parlor. She absently took note of its fine furnishings and decorations before tugging him toward a settee set close to the fireplace. Turning to close the doors tight against any curious servants, she sealed them in privacy and faced him again.

The color seemed to have returned to his handsome face, but his brows were drawn together. He leaned forward, his elbows braced on his thighs, and studied his clasped hands.

"Lord Shaston?"

He looked up, blinking as if in surprise to see her there. His beautiful blue eyes seemed to clear then, and he took in a shuddering breath.

"Miss Brianna," he murmured.

"Yes, it is I." She boldly sat beside him and covered his hands with one of hers. "Are you feeling better?"

"What?" He sat up straight. "Yes, thank you."

Lifting her hand from his, she folded her own in her lap. "Can I get you anything?"

"No." He dragged a hand through his hair. "How could you possibly know my secret?"

"I reasoned it out." She smiled at him. "You see, none of the gentlemen I spoke with this evening admitted to sending the roses. Therefore, I knew it must be you!"

He gaped at her, and then dropped his head back and barked out a laugh. "The bloody roses!"

"I do not understand. When you were not in attendance at the parties, you still owe me a dance you know, I thought it was because of my and my sister's prying this morning."

He chuckled and took her hand in his. She noted that he no longer seemed to tremble, and his grip was warm and strong.

"Forgive my reaction, Miss Brianna."

"Brianna, please."

He arched his brows, and then nodded. "Brianna. Or

may I be so bold as to call you Bree as your sister does?"

Oh, the sound of her name on his well-formed lips.

"Yes, Bree would be lovely. And there is nothing to forgive, Lord Shaston."

He shook his head. "You must call me Will."

Should she be so familiar? Oh, yes.

"Will."

His eyes lit with warmth, and he caressed her hand. "Now can you tell me why you are here at so late an hour?"

"I know it is unusual for a young woman to go to an unattached gentleman's home."

"And yet, here you are."

"My friend Patrice Prestwick divulged that her elder sister went to Lord Devlin's last Season."

"I cannot say that I am surprised, then, that they are now wed."

"They fell in love, yes." Something else occurred her, something underhanded and very unladylike indeed. "Did you think that she, that I…? Oh no, I would never think to trap a gentleman."

"I did not think so of her, and I certainly do not

think so of you."

Relief filled her at his words, said with obvious sincerity. He deserved an answer, however.

"I so thought you were my mystery suitor," she admitted in a rush.

He nodded. "I daresay, you are half right."

"What?"

"I am your suitor, I admit. But there is no mystery about my regard for you."

Her face flamed but she held his gaze. "Then you are the only suitor I want to have this Season."

He pulled back. "Do you realize what you are saying?"

"I do." She nibbled her lower lip and then nodded." I do not wish to consider any other gentlemen."

"But what of your mysterious roses, and their intriguing sender?"

She snorted. "If he can be obtuse and expect to increase my ardor by the illusion of mystery, he is not the man I desire. You are." She paused a beat. "Will."

Delight flashed across his features. "You have been the only one in my thoughts for the last two years."

It was her turn to laugh. "Other than my sister, that is. Or

Penelope Prestwick, for that matter."

He shrugged. "Merely youthful infatuations, I assure you."

"I can recognize that I am in very good company, then."

"You have not escaped my notice, Bree. Not then, and not now."

Her heart began to race as he brought his face close to hers. She closed the gap between them and pressed her lips against his. He froze for a moment, before moaning softly and taking what he had set aside last evening.

When she opened her mouth, his tongue swept in and the kiss became almost wild. His hands were firm on her waist and her stays felt tight as he pulled her against him.

"Bree." He kissed her cheek, her throat. "You are so sweet."

She had never been kissed before, and never imagined such ardor.

"Oh, Will."

He turned and suddenly she was stretched out on

the settee and he was settled comfortably over her. His clever lips trailed over her bosom until they were both breathing raggedly.

"I cannot take you," he bit out. "Christ, how I want to."

She arched toward him as his tongue teased her flesh. "Oh, my!"

Wrapping her arms around his broad back, she stroked him. She could feel the muscles bunching beneath his fine clothes and she could not resist trailing her fingers down to his taut bottom.

He growled in the back of his throat, a very sensual sound, and pressed more tightly against her. Suddenly he froze again and bolted upright.

"Damn it," he rasped, his head in his hands.

Leaning up on her elbows, she attempted to focus on him. He looked bereft as before, but instead of pale his face was now red.

"Will?"

He glanced at her, and her heart nearly broke at the sadness visible in his gaze.

"Forgive me, Bree."

She recalled the incredible feelings he had aroused with

63

his marvelous kisses and shook her head at him.

"There is nothing to forgive."

He blew out a breath. "It is true that I did not take you, but that does not discount the fact that I wanted to. That I long to still."

She tucked her legs beneath her and knelt on the settee, facing him.

"Is there such a thing as sinning in thought but not deed?"

"I do not know."

"Well, I do not believe so. You cannot convince me that anything we did this evening was wrong."

"You are naïve."

She bristled. "I am not! I may be young and still a virgin, but I am not naïve."

"I merely meant that you do not know the ways of the world. The ways of men."

Everything that her sister had gone through two years earlier, everything that her beloved brother-in-law protected their family from, flashed through her mind.

"If you knew the secrets I hold within, you would never say such a thing."

He offered her a small smile. "I will never say it again, Bree. You have my word."

She smiled back at him. "Good."

"And I will never say a word about what we discussed."

"Are you saying you will not be my suitor?"

He seemed to consider her words for a long moment before he rose and stood near the fireplace with his back to her.

"If you truly knew my secret, you would not wish me to."

She came to her feet and reached out to touch his shoulder. When he did not flinch, she counted that as a victory.

"Whatever it is, Will. Whenever you wish to share it. It will not change the way I feel about you."

He turned back to her and took her hands in his. "Then I should be the happiest of men to have your tender consideration."

Unable to resist, she touched his cheek and kissed him lightly on his lips. "You may not want it at present, but you may have anything else you might desire."

Heat flared in his gaze again and he kissed her once

more. Pressing his brow to hers, he took in a breath and slowly released it.

"I think you should go, Bree."

She nodded. "I agree."

He took one of her hands and walked with her toward the parlor doors. "I did not even ask you earlier. How did you get here?"

"My family's carriage. My aunt did not attend the parties this evening."

He smiled. "I believe the woman should keep a keener eye on you."

"There is no longer a need for that, Will. Now that we are courting, you will do that for her."

He kissed her again. "Gladly, though I fear what I might be getting into."

She laughed and he saw her to her waiting carriage.

***

Will watched her go, vastly relieved that there did not seem to be anyone else about on the street at this hour. It would not do for word of a late-night visitor to a single gentleman's home in the Earl of Lacey's carriage.

Such rumors would paint either the countess or Brianna with a very sooty brush. As it stood right now, Brianna's reputation would remain unsullied.

His heart was lighter as he returned to the parlor, but he could not ignore the disgust that had flooded him. First, when he thought Brianna knew of his past indiscretions and then when their passionate tangle had been halted by the crushing memories of it.

"God, would I ever be free of that viper?" he grumbled.

It would not touch Brianna. Never. She had been so sweet there in his arms. Her kisses, her very touch, were nothing like Lady Lasking's. That woman had been grasping, wicked, and not the least bit tender. She had left him wrung out and ashamed. There had been no satisfaction there. No true passion.

"Enough!" He poured himself another brandy and downed it in a gulp.

He would not let that hateful woman live in his mind. He was courting the sweet Brianna, and what he felt for her was desire, yes. But also protectiveness and affection. He would never have agreed to be her one and only suitor otherwise. Would he come up to snuff and feel strong enough to offer for her? He prayed it would be so.

In the bright light of morning, he set aside such dark thoughts and focused on courting the beautiful Brianna. It was far too early for him to make any sort of offer, even though he wanted her with a desire he had never before experienced. He would have to prove to himself that he could be the man she deserved, and for more than a turn about the dance floor.

He chose his clothes with care, and his valet dressed him impeccably. A charcoal gray jacket over a blue-striped waistcoat paired with a snowy white shirt. He would take his curricle today, so he donned breeches and shining boots. The small open carriage was just the thing for declaring to all and sundry that Brianna was being courted by him and him alone.

"Evan will no doubt have a field day when he learns of it," he said.

Belowstairs, he went into his study and swiftly penned a note to Brianna. He also wrote out a calling card to include with another bouquet of flowers. No doubt many other would-be suitors would send her tokens of admiration. He would have to make his stand out among them.

"Carson," he called.

The butler appeared as if through magic and bowed. "Yes, my lord?"

Will handed his note to the man. "See this letter delivered right away." He handed him the card. "Have the florist include this card in an arrangement of lilies and roses." He stilled for a moment as a thought occurred to him. "And have them add one red rose as well."

Carson was clearly holding back a smile. "Certainly."

The servant was off to do his master's bidding and Will took a breath. Hopefully he was faster than another gentleman who might presume to take her to the park this morning. Seized with a sudden feeling of urgency, he ate a small breakfast of eggs and downed a cup of coffee as he awaited her reply.

"A note has arrived for you, my lord," Carson said from the doorway.

Will took it, admiring the pretty and graceful handwriting on the foolscap. He sensed Carson still standing there and shot him a wry look.

"Is it from the young miss?" the butler asked.

"Are you going to pass gossip in the servants' hall, Carson?"

The man chuckled. "I never have before, my lord."

"It is indeed from Miss Brianna Ellsworth." He opened it and quickly read her sweet reply in the positive. "She has consented to go riding with me this morning."

Carson's brows rose clear to his hairline. "You are escorting a young lady, Lord Shaston?"

"Yes."

"To the park, I take it?"

Will nodded. "That is usually the general location for such outings."

"Are we anticipating an announcement in the near future?"

"Not the very near future, I do not believe. Soon, however. If all things go my way."

Carson grinned, a first in Will's memory. "Then I will wish you all good fortune."

Will accepted his words with a nod of his head and drained the rest of his coffee.

"Would you like anything else for breakfast, my

lord?"

"I do not dare." Will stood. "I must not keep the lady waiting."

He arrived at Lord Lacey's townhouse and was soon escorted into the foyer. The array of floral arrangements came as no surprise, and he hid his smile as he spied his own contribution. The white lilies were lush and fragrant, and the red rose a large splash of color set in the middle.

"Lord Shaston, how lovely to see you!" The countess said as she breezed into the entry.

Will took off his hat and bowed in her direction. "Good morning, Lady Lacey."

The earl entered behind her, a curious expression on his face.

"Shaston."

"Lacey," Will returned.

"You are taking Brianna to the park this morning, I take it?"

"Yes," he answered him simply.

Lacey seemed to take his measure and, when he gave a sharp nod, Will smiled.

Lady Lacey made a sound of delight and clasped her

hands together. "Let me go and get my sister."

Will and Lacey stood together now, both eyeing the floral arrangements.

"I see you sent her flowers this morning," the earl said.

"I did, yes."

"But not the red roses?"

Will saw where Lacey was pointing. There was indeed a large arrangement of blood red roses.

"No. Do you know who is sending them?"

Lacey crossed his arms. "I do not. None of us have been able to guess. Though now that you are courting our sister…?"

"I am, yes."

Lacey nodded again. "It is not very gentlemanly to attempt to excite Brianna's interest with this so-called air of mystery."

"That is my thought exactly."

"Please let us know what, if anything, you learn."

A flash of pink caught the corner of his eye, and he turned his head to find Brianna standing there beside her sister. She was even prettier than he had imagined this morning, if that was possible. Her day gown was as rosy as her cheeks as she lifted her chin and smiled at him. Her hair was upswept with a few curls framing her face, and she held a bonnet in her hands.

"Good morning, Lord Shaston."

He could not keep a grin from his face as he bowed in her direction. "Miss Brianna."

She donned the bonnet and nodded.

"Do have a good time," the countess said.

Lacey did not add his own best wishes, but he did not appear to be overly worried about their ride in the park. Will took that as a good sign. While he might not know if their courtship would end at the altar, he was pleased to know that her family trusted her in his care.

When they were out on the walk, he put his hat back on and took her hands in his. "You look beautiful as always, Bree."

"And you are at your most gallant this morning," she teased.

He shrugged. "I feared that your brother-in-law would take offense to our courtship."

"Or call you out if you did not come up to snuff?"

He blinked at her plain speaking and then chuckled, holding out a hand to assist her up into the high carriage. "I have high hopes for our connection."

She took his offered assistance, and was soon settled on the seat. He came around and joined her, taking up the leads. He began to drive the carriage toward the park.

"This is passing strange," he said.

"What is?"

"Having a young woman beside me as I ride through the park."

"It is to be a morning of firsts, then."

He glanced over at her to find that adorably sly expression on her lovely face. "Oh?"

"Yes." She settled closer to him and placed her hand around his arm. "I have never ridden through the park with a young gentleman."

He breathed in her sweet and floral scent and his mind was filled with their embrace of last evening. Or early this morning, truth be told.

"Thank you for your lovely flowers, Lord Shaston."

He arched a brow at her and she laughed softly.

"I am sorry. Thank you, Will. I almost laughed when I saw the inclusion of that lone red rose."

"I knew you would see the significance. I believe I saw yet another bouquet of red roses in the entry."

"Yes, they came again. I do wish whoever was sending them would either reveal himself or take himself off."

"I admit I hope the latter."

"Why?"

"I would not like to compete with yet another suitor."

She snuggled a little closer. "I have no other suitor, remember?"

The conviction in which she said it made him wish for a moment that he could feel confident enough to go to her sister and brother-in-law and formally request her hand. Perhaps before this Season is over.

He could not resist winking at her.

"I am very pleased to hear that, Bree."

Chapter 5

Brianna felt a flush at Will's words. He looked so handsome today. She longed to get even closer to him. Her gaze fell to his lips. To perhaps kiss him again? There was no way he would allow such a thing, not as they headed into the crowded park.

"Here we go," he said in a low voice. "Brace yourself."

She giggled and sat up straight by his side. His shoulders were so broad that as he expertly maneuvered the curricle he brushed against her side. The preferred track of the park was crowded with carriages and horses, but Will confidently worked the reins. As they made their way, she could see heads turning their way.

"We are attracting attention," she murmured.

"Does that worry you?"

She shook her head. "Not in the least."

Merging into the line of carriages, they slowed to a veritable crawl as expected. Will squared his impressive shoulders as a group of gentlemen approached on horseback.

"Shaston!" Lord Wilbrey called. "And do I see the

lovely Miss Brianna Ellsworth?"

"You do indeed," Will answered him.

The blond gentleman bowed his head to her. "You look a vision, Miss Brianna."

"Thank you, Lord Wilbrey."

His eyes sparkled as he raised his brows at Will. "The park is quite crowded this morning, Shaston."

"I am counting on that, Wilbrey," he answered.

Evan looked about and then grinned at Will. "A couple of clucking hens are headed your way."

Brianna blinked in confusion and Will leaned close again. "Lords Bottom and Erlington."

She saw them then, two stout gentlemen perched on top of their mounts. They both eyed her closely and she fought the urge to slink down in her seat. There was nothing untoward about their expressions, as humor crinkled their eyes. Still, she read the speculation in their gazes.

"Ho, Shaston!" Lord Bottom said.

"Well, well," Lord Erlington said. "Miss Brianna Ellsworth is seated here beside you, and as pretty as ever."

Brianna dipped her head at the two gentlemen. Will did not appear the least bit jealous of their attention, which she herself could understand. With him beside her, she would be hard-pressed to consider any other gentleman.

"Fellows," Will returned. "Indeed, the beautiful Miss Brianna is my chosen partner as of this morning."

Partner? Brianna wondered at his wording but, when the other two men's mouth dropped open, she gathered they grasped his meaning.

"Is this way of things, then?" Lord Bottom laughed out loud. "I cannot say I am surprised."

"You do have all the luck, Shaston," Lord Erlington said.

She did not catch any true discomfort from either of them, even though they circled around all of the young ladies at the parties.

"I daresay we will not be fortunate enough to claim a dance with you this evening, then?" Lord Bottom asked.

She gave a tiny shake of her head and the two men chuckled again.

"Quite right," Lord Erlington said with a smile.

They bowed their heads and continued on their way as Will held firmly to the reins.

"There," he said softly.

She turned to him. "Are you talking to me or to the horses?" she teased.

He laughed. "Both, I think. We can trust those two to spread the word of our very new connection."

She thought for a moment. "Hmm."

"What are you thinking, or do I wish to know?"

She took a breath and slowly let it out. "Oh, I was merely considering if I feel any sort of regret now that no other gentleman save you shall dance with me."

"And? What is your conclusion?"

He did appear a little bit worried, which pleased her to her toes.

"I can ascertain no such regrets."

The smile he gave her was bright and handsome and she surely would have swooned had she not been seated so close to him.

"I will miss the flowers, though," she laughed.

He clicked his tongue and playfully shook his head at her.

"I think that from now on, you may still count on receiving flowers."

She was about to ask him his thoughts about the red roses when Lord Wilbrey approached once more

"Shaston and Miss Brianna," he said as he reined in his horse beside them. "A matched pair in my friend's curricle pulled by an equally matched pair."

His words were silly, and she was surprised to see this lighter side of him. He always seemed so reserved previously.

"Hello, Lord Wilbrey," she said brightly.

He smiled and dipped his head. "Are you enjoying your ride with our mutual friend?"

"Friend?" Will cut in.

Lord Wilbrey splayed a hand on his chest. "Best friend, truth be told. Miss Brianna, you are in good hands with Lord Shaston."

"I agree wholeheartedly with you, Lord Wilbrey," she said.

Will shook his head at his friend. "What are you about this morning, Wilbrey?"

The man's brows rose in mock innocence. "I am merely paying my regards, Shaston."

There seemed to be no animosity between the two

of them, which was nice to see.

"I am certain that my friend here will claim all of your dances, so may I say that I am looking forward to seeing the two of you this evening."

"Thank you, Lord Wilbrey."

He shared a look of some import with Will before making his farewells and riding past them.

"Are you good friends with Lord Wilbrey?" she asked.

"I am, yes. He knows just about all of my secrets."

"I see. But no secret about red roses, I take it?"

"No." He smiled. "I promise we shall get to the bottom of that particular secret."

His words reminded her that just last night he had blanched when she had mentioned his secret. What could he be hiding?

"Lord Shaston, when I first um, approached you last evening, I mentioned something about a secret."

His lips thinned. "Yes, you did."

She leaned closer. "Then you do have a secret?" she whispered.

He appeared troubled for a long moment, but then he nodded. "I do, but it is not something to divulge, especially to you."

She blinked. What could it possibly be?

"You would have my utmost discretion," she assured him.

He covered her hands with one of his. "I know. Perhaps one day I can tell you."

"Tell her what?" Mr. Stilling barked from his position beside the carriage.

Will once more held to the reins. "Hello, Stinky."

Brianna hid her smile at the oft-heard nickname. "Hello, Mr. Stilling."

"I daresay you are the prettiest young lady in the park, Miss Brianna."

"She is, indeed," Will said. "And she is riding with me."

"Yes." Mr. Stilling said. "This is a new development, is it not?"

"Now Mr. Stilling, it is not very gallant of you to speak of this," she cheekily admonished.

His cheeks flushed red and he scowled at her. Here was the spoiled gentleman she remembered from when he had courted Marianne two years past.

"As you say," he bit out. "I bid you both good day, then."

He was gone as quickly as traffic on the track would allow and Will laughed softly.

"He is quite amusing," she observed.

"And you delivered quite the dressing down."

"Is that not done?" she asked.

"Oh, it is done. I was merely considering just how pleased I am that you approve of my suit."

Disregarding the curious eyes all around them, she tucked her hand into the crook of his arm and smiled.

"I approve wholeheartedly, Will."

The rest of the morning went in a similar fashion, and the ride back to Lord Lacey's house was all too short. His carriage bounced in a delightful fashion as he pulled the reins to a stop.

"Thank you for a lovely ride," she said.

He leaned closer to her. "Thank you for the company."

She breathed in deeply of his scent. Her heart began to race, and she thought for a moment that he would kiss her. Instead, he gracefully stepped down from the carriage and walked around to hold out one hand to assist her. Taking it, she carefully alighted and allowed him to accompany her up the front steps. The door was swiftly opened by the butler and she and Will were once again in the foyer.

"May I expect to see you at the parties this evening?" he asked.

"Oh, yes."

His pretty blue eyes sparkled. "I look forward to them with much anticipation." He buzzed a kiss to her knuckles. "Until tonight, then."

He sketched a bow and left. She leaned against the open door, her limbs trembling from simply being near him.

"Do I regret that no other gentleman will dance with me?" she mused aloud. A big grin spread across her face. "Not in the least!"

Humming to herself, she removed her bonnet and gloves and went in search of her sister.

***

After leaving Brianna safely at Lacey's home, Will decided to spar at the athletic club. It had been a long time since he had a good match, and he had an easy time finding partners. One in particular was a rather large and congenial man, with only a few teeth missing from his winning smile.

Will stepped toward the ring wearing his breeches and holding a towel. He found the man, Joseph, just stepping out of the ring. His previous partner, a gentleman Will knew only in passing, nodded his flushed face as he made his way toward the benches.

"Lord Shaston, looking for a beating today?" Joseph said to Will.

"Joseph, do your worst."

Joseph laughed. "If you insist. I assume you don't want me to mess up that pretty face of yours?"

Will chuckled and set his towel down. "I do prefer that, please."

Joseph rubbed his big meaty hands together and then waved Will into the ring with a grin. "After you, my lord."

Will joined him and, after about twenty minutes of getting sweaty, and getting his chest and belly pummeled, he'd had enough. He held up a hand and braced the other on a knee as he sought to catch his breath.

"Excellent match, Joseph," he said at last.

Joseph, who aside from flushed cheeks looked none the

worse for wear, dipped his head.

"Always a pleasure."

Will stepped out of the ring and made his way toward the pitchers and basins of water set out for the participants. He splashed his face and toweled off before straightening.

"You looked good in the ring," someone said to his side.

Will eyed the man he now recognized from the pub a few nights ago. He nodded his acknowledgment.

"Don't know how well you would do in a real fight," the man went on.

Will ran his eyes over him now. In this light he seemed a few years older than Will, and a little more broadly built. He was neither homely nor handsome in his opinion.

"See here, what is your problem with me?"

The man placed his hands on his hips. "Nothing with you in particular, mind. Just your kind in general."

"My kind?"

"You nobles. Noses in the air all the time, even when you're riding through the park."

Something niggled at the back of Will's mind. Had he seen him in the park the other morning?

"Do you often ride through the park yourself?" Will asked.

The other man sniffed. "Are you saying I don't have the right to?"

"No." Will shook his head. "I do not want to argue with you, sir."

The man removed his shirt and made his way toward the ring. "As you say."

With that, he seemed to dismiss Will. Will watched his retreating back and wondered if his ire extended solely due to their argument in the pub or was it something deeper?

He rode back home to change and eat something for luncheon before heading back out to his gentlemen's club. His interaction with the prickly gentleman, as he thought of him now, stayed with him. He was almost certain he had seen him in the park the other morning as he had spoken to Brianna and her sister. Could that be his issue with him in particular, despite his words to the contrary?

"Just your kind," Will muttered. "Strange fellow."

"Who?" Evan asked as he joined him.

Will glanced up and shrugged. "No one of import, I daresay. Just a prickly gentleman at the ring today."

Evan laughed. "Did he beat you in the ring?"

Will laughed, and then rubbed a sore spot on his belly. "No, but Joseph gave me a sound thrashing."

"He always does."

Evan grabbed a pack of playing cards from the center of the table and sat across from him. "Now what is this about a prickly gentleman?"

He began to deal the cards and Will mused over the question.

"I ran into him at a pub the other night, also. He was rude to one of the serving women and I called him on it."

"That was your first mistake."

"No, the owner backed me up and had him escorted out."

"And that, I would guess, was your second."

"I suppose." Will looked absently at his hand of cards. "Today, he spoke of a problem with 'our kind.' Nobles with our noses in the air even as we ride through the park."

Evan blinked. "That seems oddly specific."

"I thought so as well. That is when I remembered that I thought I saw him the other morning."

Evan shrugged then. "The park is a veritable crush this time of year, Will."

"Yes, but he had seemed almost furtive."

"Furtive?"

"Yes. On the fringes of the crowd and watching as I spoke with Brianna."

"Hmm." Evan suddenly brightened. "Hold on a moment. Brianna?"

"That is her name."

"Yes, I believe that you are now visibly courting her so perhaps the gentleman was jealous?"

Will huffed out a breath. "Even if he was, it was odd behavior. Bottom and Erlington merely teased me before acknowledging my suit."

"Was anyone else about?"

"Stinky Stilling."

"Ho, I imagine he was beyond jealous."

"He may have been, but he has no right to be. Chasing the earl's wife before turning his attention to Brianna."

Evan threw him a flat look, and Will chuckled.

"All right, I was enamored of Lady Lacey as well. I blame youth."

"I shall allow it. I was one of those heartbroken swains too, you know."

Will smiled at his friend. "I do."

They half-heartedly played a two-handed game of whist for a while before Will placed his cards on the table.

"I wonder, Evan."

"What do you wonder?"

"Who has been sending Brianna those red roses?"

"It must be someone we have not yet considered. What about your prickly gentleman?"

"I do not know if he even knows her."

"Did you not say he was watching as you spoke with her?"

"Yes. I wish now I had asked his name."

"Ask Joseph the next time you go in for a beating."

Will thought for a moment. "I believe I shall. Capital idea, Evan."

Evan bowed his head. "I do my best. It seems that

you are making up for lost time, staking your claim on Miss Brianna so early in the Season."

Will's stomach churned but he held his countenance. "Lost time?"

"You left in a hurry last year, Will. Did something happen?"

Will blew out a breath. "I still cannot speak of it."

"You seemed to be having a pleasant Season, were you not? I believe you were even considering romancing the Prestwick girl."

"Devlin's wife, you mean," Will said without pique. "That match was a *fait accompli*."

Evan nodded. "Too true. Was it another young lady who broke your tender heart, then?"

"It was no young lady," Will said in a low voice. "And my heart was not the least bit involved."

Evan blinked, and then his mouth dropped open. "Never say you tangled with a certain... I cannot think of a word for her."

Will just looked at his friend until Evan let out a low whistle.

"It is rumored that she plays for keeps, friend. How the

devil did you escape with your, um, self-respect intact?"

Will studied the table. "I barely did, believe me."

Evan leaned back. "You did not have to leave Town, Will. I would have helped you had I but known."

Will looked up and shook his head. "There was nothing you could do." He recalled the first time he debased himself with Lady Lasking. "She is not some great seductress," he rasped.

Evan's brow furrowed. "Are you saying that she…"

Will leaned toward his friend. "Forced me, yes."

"I am sorry, Will." Evan placed a hand on Will's arm. "You were right to leave Town."

"It was the only way I could think of to end it." He closed his eyes. "I would not wish her attentions on my worst enemy."

"Have you noticed any marked attention from her this Season?"

"The bitch has been writing me."

"She is still enamored of you?"

Will shook his head. "I sincerely doubt she is pining over me. I think it is a matter of her pride at this point."

"And there is no chance of her success?"

"Not even in the slightest."

"I am relieved to hear that, friend." Evan grew thoughtful. "I daresay you have chosen the perfect woman for you, then."

Will thought of sweet Brianna, her freshness and open character, and nodded. "I agree. She has a streak of rebelliousness in her, however."

Evan's brows rose. "How so?"

"She came to my home last evening."

"Never say that you and she…"

"No!" Will looked about and lowered his voice. "No, of course not."

"There is something you are not telling me."

"She believed it was I sending the unmarked red roses."

"Well, she looked quite pleased with her choice of suitor this morning, so I take it she was not disappointed to learn it was not you?"

Will could not keep the grin from his face. "She was not."

"And now you are courting her?"

"I am."

"And here we are, not a month into the new Season. Will you marry?"

"That, I do not know at present."

Evan slid him a grin.

"What?" Will asked.

"It just seems to me that Devlin said the very same thing last year."

Will caught his meaning and laughed. He knew, however, that there were worse things that could happen than being betrothed to his Brianna.

Chapter 6

Brianna once more stood with Patrice Prestwick at a crowded ball, but it seemed as though matters were vastly different from just two nights ago. Riding with Will this morning, to and from the park and all of the delectable interactions in between, still made her tingle. They had been sitting so close, her hand tucked in the crook of one of his strong arms, and it had felt so right.

"You have made up your mind, I take it?" Patrice asked.

Brianna blinked and turned to face her friend. "My mind?"

Patrice grinned and leaned closer. "Lord Shaston is your choice."

Brianna could not help smiling herself. "He is, yes."

"And he is courting you now?"

"He is."

"Has he offered for you?"

"No! It is far too early for that."

"I suppose. But last Season Lord Devlin did not waste a moment before securing the affections of my sister."

Brianna did not know the particulars of Penelope's courtship with Lord Devlin, but she supposed they did connect very soon after the Season had commenced.

"They do appear to be quite happy, Patrice. Nearly as happy as my dear sister and brother-in-law."

"Very much so." Patrice swayed to the music for a moment as she perused the gathering. "Has he kissed you?"

"Patrice!" Brianna's cheeks flamed but she nodded.

Patrice's eyes grew round. "Brianna!"

"Shh!" Brianna rolled her eyes. "You would think this was your first Season."

"Well, as I still have not had my first kiss I feel as though it is."

"You have plenty of suitors."

"But you have the one."

A little thrill went through her. "I do."

"And that is what you will be saying very soon, I wager."

"Really, Patrice." Brianna clicked her tongue. "A lady does not wager."

The two of them fell to laughing.

"My, my," a man said to their right. "Pray, what

amuses you both so?"

Brianna saw it was Lord Wilbrey and dropped a curtsey. "Hello, Lord Wilbrey."

Patrice grew quiet, a very unusual condition for a Prestwick lady to exhibit.

"You both look quite lovely this evening," Lord Wilbrey said. "Miss Patrice, I would much desire to secure a dance with you this evening. May I count upon it?"

While Patrice made some sort of sound of consent, Brianna spotted Will making his impressive way in her direction. The elegant surroundings faded from her notice as he neared. She clasped her hands together to keep them from fluttering all around. Why was she being such a ninny? They had been alone together just this morning, after all. And last night in his home!

"Miss Brianna," he said with a dip of his head.

"Lord Shaston," she managed to return.

"You look almost as beautiful under these chandeliers as you did this morning in the bright sunshine."

Brianna waved away his compliment. "I much enjoyed our ride this morning."

"Oh, did the two of you see each other this morning?"

Lord Wilbrey raised his brows at Patrice. "Have you heard of this, Miss Patrice?"

She blinked and then nodded vigorously. "Why yes, Lord Wilbrey. I believe they were in the park together this very morning."

Brianna took a breath and shared a warm look with Will.

"Have you come to claim your dance, Lord Shaston?" she asked.

He grinned and held his arm out to her. "The first of many this evening, I hope."

She nodded and placed her hand on his arm as they glided onto the dance floor. They were separated with regularity due to the nature of the particular dance, and whenever they came back together her heart raced. It was amazing, this reaction she had to Will. They had only shared a few heated kisses in his front parlor, yet the memory of his hungry lips on her skin caused her to flush.

His gaze never seemed to leave hers as they met one last time. For a moment, he pulled her close and seemed to breathe in with a sound of contentment. Oh, his scent flooded her senses as well.

"May I suggest foregoing a second dance at present?" he asked softly.

She raised her gaze to his face. "The terrace, my lord?"

He growled softly and then stepped a proper distance away from her. "Would you enjoy a stroll, Miss Brianna?"

"I would, Lord Shaston. Very much so."

As they left the dance floor something from the back of the ballroom caught her eye. It was a gentleman who kept his face turned toward the wall, but she could just make out his profile. He looked very familiar, but she could not place him.

"Bree?" Will asked to her left.

"Hmm?" She turned back to Will. "Pardon?"

"You appeared distracted." Will blinked down at her. "Is something troubling you?"

She glanced back toward that corner of the room but did not see the gentleman now. She smiled up at Will.

"No, Will. How could anything trouble me while I am on your arm?"

He chuckled as they continued on toward the terrace. Coming to the iron railing, they stood very close together. Their hands touched and she wished that she did not wear gloves. Still, when he covered her hand with his, she could feel his warmth and strength.

"You look very beautiful this evening, Bree."

She turned just slightly to edge closer to him. "You are the most handsome man here."

"I have missed you."

She smiled. "We were together just this morning."

"What can I say? It feels like days more than hours."

She could not ignore the way his words seemed to wrap around her. "You do not have to say such things."

"I do, as they are true."

"Is this because you are my suitor now?"

He appeared thoughtful and then smiled again. "I am your only suitor, and I only speak the truth. Did you not miss me?"

Her cheeks flushed hot. "I did. What does that make me?"

He leaned very close, nearly touching his brow to hers. "That makes you mine."

"Oh, I wish I was daring enough to come to your townhouse again this evening."

Heat flared in his gaze. "That would be dangerous."

"Are you afraid of me, Lord Shaston?"

"Not in the least. The danger, my dear Miss Brianna, comes completely from myself."

"We are courting," she reasoned aloud.

His nostrils flared and his chest expanded as he seemed to draw her in. "We are, indeed."

"Then perhaps I may have another headache coming on."

He came closer, his lips tantalizingly close to hers. "I want to taste you again."

She hesitated a beat, and then came up on her toes to press her lips to his. His arms came around her and he kissed her far more deeply than he had the last time they had been together on a terrace. His tongue swept into her mouth and for a breathless moment she was very close to swooning there on the flagstones. Voices reached her and, in a flash, he separated from her and stared out at the gardens.

Another couple strolled by, and she and Will nodded their greetings.

"You will be the death of me," he murmured.

She could not help but laugh at his words. "The gardens

look lovely."

He glanced out at the paths lit by lanterns placed few and far between. "It does appear to be a pleasant space."

She gladly put her hand on his offered arm as they took the few steps down to the relative seclusion of the gardens. The scent of jasmine was heavy here, and she took a moment to simply breathe. The gardens themselves were nothing out of the ordinary, especially compared to those at her brother-in-law's townhouse, but it did give them the opportunity to speak more freely.

The gravel crunched beneath her slippers as they made their way along the winding paths. The pretty iron lanterns were lit but their light was not cast very far from their posts. They strolled in and out of the circles of light as they moved farther away from the terrace.

"Is your company promised to any other gentlemen this evening?" he asked.

"Any others?"

"You were here for a time before my arrival."

"I take it you believe me so fickle as to lose interest, Will?"

He cupped her cheek, stroking her with his thumb. "I do not, but that is not to say that I doubt the enthusiasm of certain gentlemen."

"Perhaps your good friend Lord Wilbrey?"

His thumb brushed her lips before he dropped his hand. "Wilbrey is well aware of our situation and would never dare anything so scandalous as to court a lady already secured."

"Am I truly secured?"

"I have not asked formally, but that is only because it is so early in the Season."

She thought of last Season, when he had disappeared so suddenly. "May I count on you to remain in Town this Season?"

A pained expression flashed across his features, gone in a moment. "You may."

She longed to ask him what was troubling him, as his expression put her in mind of his reaction when she had first arrived at his townhouse, but she could not bear to cause him any more discomfort.

"Then consider me secured."

***

He glanced about and led her out of the meager circle of

light provided by the small lantern above. They were shrouded in near dark and, from the sly expression on her beautiful face, he believed she was very daring indeed to be in the gardens with him tonight.

"Kiss me, Will."

He pulled her close again and was certain that she could feel every bit of his body pressed to hers.

"You tempt me, Bree."

"If I am yours, then you are also mine. There is no temptation here."

He growled again, giving up the struggle for a blessed moment, and he captured her lips again. As his tongue entered her mouth, she touched it with hers and the sensation inflamed him. His mouth moved to the side of her neck, and she gasped as it grew bolder. He dropped kisses on her bosom and one touch to the front of her dress told him her hardened nipples ached for more direct contact than he could provide at present. When his hands cupped her bottom and began to knead her flesh, she nearly shouted her pleasure.

"Bree." He ran his hands over her back now. "Christ, I want you."

His cock hardened against her belly. He was certain that she was pure, but surely she had gathered enough from her sister's passionate marriage to know something about this kind of closeness. He reasoned that her sister had told her precious little about the physical act itself, of course. To his delight and surprise, she moved one delicate hand between them and stroked his chest down to his belly. For one heart-stopping moment he waited for the familiar shame to swamp him, but her touch was tender and nothing like before. He took her hand and held it to his shaft before bringing her hand to his lips.

"You put me in a difficult position," he rasped, his breath labored.

"You are making me melt, so we are even."

"We cannot do this." He kissed her again and stepped back. "Not here."

She fanned herself with one hand as she patted her hair. "No, not here."

He knew he should not presume, but he needed her. "I can keep you safe, you know."

"Safe?" Her confusion was charming but was swiftly replaced with acute interest. "My heart or my virtue?"

He cupped her flushed cheek as he had earlier. "Both."

That sly smile curved her full lips and she held a hand to her brow. "Oh, I do believe I am developing a headache."

He caught her meaning and took a few deep breaths to cool his ardor. "Then let me return you to the ballroom to give your farewells to our host and hostess."

"Thank you, Lord Shaston."

He held her hand where it rested on his arm, doing his best to keep her at a respectable distance. As they reentered the ballroom, he glanced about and saw that no one was paying them any pointed attention. His gaze settled on Lord Wilbrey, where he stood with Patrice Prestwick. Evan's eyes sparkled, and he wore a smirk as Will and Brianna approached.

"I daresay I must give my regrets to our host and hostess," Brianna said.

There was nothing in her tone that seemed insincere, and Will had to refrain from smirking himself.

"You should go right home," Miss Patrice said. "But you do not have Lord Lacey's carriage tonight."

"Hmm, that is true," Brianna said.

"May I drive you home?" Will asked.

"Oh no, I could not ask that of you. I shall have a hack called."

"I shall call one for you." Will took her hands in his. "And wait with you out front."

"Thank you, Lord Shaston."

Miss Patrice narrowed her eyes, but the convoluted tale was believable enough. She grinned and nodded vigorously. Brianna dipped a curtsey and left them. As she skirted the crowded dance floor, Will thought he spotted the strange gentleman from the athletic club. He turned to Evan to catch his attention but when he turned back the man was no longer there. Had he imagined him?

"Evan," he said softly.

His friend perked up and faced him. "What is it, Will?"

"Did you see that dark-haired man in the corner there?"

Evan's eyes narrowed as he scanned that part of the ballroom. "I do not see anyone I do not know." He lowered his voice. "The prickly gentleman?"

Will nodded as he too looked over the faces of the other partygoers. There was no sign of him that he could see. Had he imagined him?

"I shall keep out a weather eye," Evan said. "Perhaps you should head home?" he added on a whisper.

Will nodded to his friend. "I believe you may be correct."

Will flagged down a servant and instructed them to call a hack for Brianna. Then it was Will's turn to bid his host and hostess farewell and board his carriage headed back to his townhouse. He thought of his and Brianna's heated embrace in the darkened gardens. There had been no shame or disgust, to his great relief. Just sweet Brianna and pure desire.

Would she truly come to his townhouse later that evening? She was daring enough for anything. He knew this and silently vowed, as he had told her earlier, to protect her and keep her safe.

Carson was waiting for him when he arrived home as no surprise.

"You are home early, my lord."

"As you see, Carson." He took off his hat and handed it to the butler. "Has anyone called?"

"Called, Lord Shaston?"

Will arched a brow and Carson shook his head. "Not as of yet, my lord."

"You and the others may turn in, I daresay. I shall stay up in the parlor." He cleared his throat. "Reading."

"Reading, yes."

Did Carson know what he had planned? The butler wore a sober expression as he did most of the time, but Will would wager he suspected plenty. No matter. He would see Brianna this evening with no one around to discover them and ruin her reputation.

The butler left him, and Will went into the parlor. "One would think I often had young ladies here," he marveled aloud.

He removed his jacket and poured himself a brandy. His mind was fully on the coming encounter. He had not yet offered for her. That was true. She would be the perfect bride for him, though. Of that, he was certain. Would she accept him after she knew his secret? Of that, he was less sure.

Not ten minutes had passed when he heard a now-familiar light knocking. He opened the door and found Brianna on the porch once again. He could not keep the smile from his face as he took her hand and tugged her inside. He managed to keep from kissing her until he had her safely ensconced in the front parlor.

Taking both of her hands now, bare of the gloves she had worn earlier, he bent his head and captured her lips. She tasted even sweeter than she had earlier.

"I feared that you would beat me here," he said, taking her light cloak from her shoulders. "My butler would have been scandalized."

She smiled and shook her head. "I asked the driver to proceed very slowly."

He laughed and held her close. "You have more patience than I."

She threw her arms around his neck. "I find I have very little patience where it comes to you."

Their current position brought her body flush with his. He hardened in an instant.

"I could hardly wait to hold you in my arms again, Bree."

"You said you wanted me, Will." She kissed his neck, a sweet and sensual caress. "There in the garden."

"I did." He ran his hands over her curves.

Everywhere he touched seemed to burn him in the best possible way. "I do."

She arched as he cupped her breast. "Take me, Will."

He paused for but a moment before spreading her on the settee beneath him. He braced himself on his elbows and kissed her softly.

"I will not take you, Bree. But I shall endeavor to give you pleasure."

She touched his face and gazed up at him. "You promised to keep me safe."

"And I shall."

He kissed her again, their tongues tangling as he slowly stroked one hand up her leg. There was a froth of skirts between them, but he unerringly sought his treasure. Where her stockings met her skin, she was silky smooth. The heat of her struck him as he came tantalizingly close to her pussy.

"Oh, Will." Her thighs spread a bit as he began to tease her. "Oh, my!"

He nuzzled her cheek, her throat, as he made his way to her breasts. Leaning on one elbow, he tugged down her bodice and freed one nipple. It was pink and pert, and he could not resist its temptation. He closed his mouth over her and suckled.

She gasped and cradled his head, running her fingers through his hair as she held him willing captive. Her innocence was clear but so was her passion. This embrace held no resemblance to what he had experienced last summer. That was certain. He suspected that he could have stripped her bare in this moment and made her fully his, but he had promised to keep her safe and he would do his damnedest to keep that promise.

"I want you, Bree," he told her again as he kissed the sweet valley between her breasts. "I want to bring you to the pinnacle of pleasure."

She made a sound of assent and arched upward. He teethed her nipple as he teased her beneath her skirts. Slipping a finger beneath the hem of her drawers, he found her wet and willing. It took but a few strokes to her center before she was cresting on what he was certain was her very first orgasm.

Her cries were sweet, and he held her there until she at last stilled. He removed his hand at last and gazed down at her. When she opened her eyes, he could see the satisfaction on her flushed and beautiful face.

"Will, that was amazing."

"God, love." He kissed her and smiled. "You are even more beautiful in your passion, Bree."

"You called me 'love,' Will." She touched his cheek. "No one has ever done so."

The address felt right somehow, even this early in their attachment.

"I did, yes. I have never called any woman that before."

"I believe you." Her cheeks turned pink now. "No one has ever touched…me."

"Then I am the most fortunate of men."

She placed a hand on his chest and stroked down to his belly. "I want to touch you."

He held her hand and pressed it to the front of his trousers. "You can feel how much I want you, but you are innocent."

"That does not mean I cannot give you pleasure too."

When she licked her lips, he nearly came at the thought of her mouth on him. He knew full well that had not been her meaning, however. Sitting back, he took a deep breath in an attempt to cool himself.

"Just give me a few minutes to collect myself. I will be

all right."

She came to her knees and adjusted her bodice matter-of-factly, hiding her magnificent breasts from view once more. "I daresay you shall be a sight more than all right."

Chapter 7

Brianna watched as passion once more lit Will's gaze. His touch, his kisses, had thrilled her yet he was still visibly aroused. She might not know much but she reasoned she would be able to ease him at the very least.

After a few fumbles, she unbuttoned and opened his waistcoat and shirt to reveal a bit of his smooth and muscular chest. His skin was warm to the touch, and she could not resist stroking him.

"You are very beautiful, Will."

He smiled crookedly at her. "If you insist, though just the smallest bits of you I have seen far exceed anything."

Her fingers danced over his flat, ridged belly, and then she attempted to free him from his breeches. Chuckling, he deftly unfastened his buttons and she took a moment to study him. His shaft was long and thick, and unlike anything she had ever encountered. One touch to it and he hissed.

"Does that hurt?" she asked.

He leaned his head back and closed his eyes. "God, no. Your touch is amazing."

Mirroring what he had done to her, she kissed him and nuzzled his throat as she stroked her hand over his length. His fresh, hot scent was stronger where she rubbed her face against his chest. She turned her head and his heart pounded beneath her ear as she continued to tease his manhood.

She was unschooled and felt utterly inept, until he covered her hand with his. They moved together then, faster and faster until Will was bucking on the settee. At the very last, when she was certain something was about to happen, he held himself close to his belly and groaned with his release. Her hand felt a bit sticky, but she could not resist kissing him again.

When he caught his breath, he smiled at her. "Your touch, Bree. It is like no other."

She sat back on her heels. "Then, I pleased you? With your help, that is?"

He laughed and hugged her to him. "You pleased me very well indeed!"

She glanced at the wetness on his belly and then back at his face. "You kept me safe."

"Yes, but I was not inside of you."

She gasped and he cursed softly. She watched in amazement as he tucked himself away and buttoned his shirt.

"Forgive me, Bree. I should not have spoken so freely to someone as innocent as you."

That brought to mind the many women he must have been with in his bachelorhood. It was a dark thought, and she had trouble setting it from her mind. Apparently, he caught something in her demeanor, for he gently touched her arm.

"What is it?" he asked.

She could not face him as she asked but she needed to know, so she dropped her gaze to her hands. "How many women have you been with, then?"

"Not very many," he stated.

"And none of them were innocent?"

"None of them were pure, no."

"Oh." She thought back to that first night she arrived at his home. "I thought that was your secret."

He stilled and he removed his hand and held it in a fist. "My secret?"

"Yes, that you have had many innocent young ladies."

When he fell silent, she looked up at him again. She was surprised to find his brow furrowed.

"What is wrong, Will?"

He ran his hands through his hair and leaned forward to rest his arms on his thighs. "I have a secret, but there is nothing innocent about it."

Tucking her legs beneath her, she knelt beside him and placed a hand on his shoulder.

"Your secret will be safe with me," she promised.

He blew out a breath, and then glanced at her. "As safe as I will keep your heart?"

She shrugged. "I certainly hope so."

He seemed to be gathering his strength, and she could only assume that it was difficult for him.

"Last Season, Bree." He hesitated. "I had several encounters with someone who was not very kind."

Her mind worked. "Are you saying they hurt you?"

He shook his head. "No. Not really. But they were not in the least bit tender and would not heed my refusal."

Her mouth dropped open. "They forced you."

He shot her a look. "How could you know of such things?"

Sadly, she did know. And that a cruel person had forced themselves on the dearest person she knew.

"Well, it is not my secret to tell but I know someone who was very ill-used. It nearly ruined her life."

Would he guess she spoke of her sister? She prayed it would not be so.

"I am ashamed of what became of me last summer, Bree. That is why I left so suddenly."

She stroked his arm, soothing him now as she had aroused him earlier. "You have no cause to feel ashamed, Will. If someone takes advantage of you, that is their sin. Not yours."

He faced her fully, his eyes beseeching hers. "Do you truly believe that?"

She nodded. "I do. And as I said before, your secret is safe with me."

His features smoothed and he gave her a small smile. "You are amazing, Bree."

"Then it is very good that you have chosen to court me this Season."

The touch of levity was just enough to brighten his face. He hugged her to him, and then they began to kiss again. He pulled away and stared at her, passion and affection clear in his gaze. Her heart raced and suddenly she knew she would do just about anything he desired of her. If that meant giving him her virtue, so be it.

"I know it has only been a few days, but what would you say if I went to your sister and brother-in-law?"

She blinked. "To formally ask for my hand?"

"Yes."

This, she had not been expecting. "Pardon?"

He took her hands then, stroking his thumbs over her knuckles. "I would never be able to find another with so sweet a heart as yours."

She thought furiously for a long moment. He was everything she could desire. He would no doubt provide well for her and help her give her sister the privacy she deserved and remove her as a burden. As for herself, she wanted him like she had never desired another gentleman.

"If you are certain," was all she could say.

He beamed a beautiful smile at her and held her close. "Thank you."

The relief in his voice was clear and she ran her hand over his back. "You are everything good, Will.

Believe that."

He pulled back and kissed her lightly. "I know not how long matters can take to arrange."

A delicious thought occurred to her. "Well, as your betrothed I am telling you that I will not wait to share more than we did this evening."

He gaped at her, and then tipped his head back and laughed.

"God, love. I believe you may just be my perfect match."

He clasped his hands around her waist and drew her onto his lap. "I want you more than anything, but I will try my utmost to be the man you deserve."

Her throat tightened at his apparent doubt in his own character.

"Will, you already are."

He moved to kiss her again before setting her away from him.

"You are too much of a temptation," he playfully grumbled.

She came to her feet as steadily as she could manage and lifted her chin. "I choose to believe that is a good thing."

"Ah, it is a very good thing," he said with a smile.

Then he stood as well, holding his hands at his sides as if to restrain himself from taking her in his arms once more.

"Let us get you safely home, Bree. Then I shall think on what might be the best manner in which to approach Lord and Lady Lacey."

She longed to stay, to throw any sort of propriety left to her out the fine leaded windows onto the streets of Mayfair. Instead, she stood demurely as he placed her cloak on her shoulders.

He dropped a kiss on her cheek. "Let me call for a hack."

She soon found herself on her way back to her brother-in-law's townhouse. Her insides were aquiver, not only with the delicious pleasures they had explored this evening but with the knowledge that he would soon be her betrothed!

"Wait until Patrice Prestwick hears of this," she sighed.

***

Will watched the hack leave as he had done earlier, and then closed the door. He turned to find Carson standing in the entry.

"My lord?"

Will smiled at the elderly butler. "Are you about to raise the alarm and declare me a debaucher of innocent young ladies?"

"Are you?"

"Carson, I will assure you that I am going to marry that particular innocent young lady."

A smile broke out on the servant's face. "That is wonderful news, my lord."

"I believe so."

"Then, we can expect you to remain in Town?"

Will could guess to what the man alluded. He had been a close witness to Will's dour condition and discomfort on several evenings last Season. They never spoke of it, and would not this evening, but Will knew Carson only spoke out of concern.

"I and my new wife, whenever we are able to see the deed done, shall live here through the Season."

Carson's brows drew together. "What of your family, my lord?"

Will thought for a moment. "I will write my sister and

have her relay the news to my mother, I think."

"Yes, I daresay that may be the best way to handle your news. Um, precisely when might we have the news officially?"

"I am asking for her hand on the morrow, Carson."

"And you are certain of your acceptance?"

"Lord and Lady Lacey take prodigious good care of Miss Brianna, but I do believe they will accept my offer."

Carson grinned now. "Capital!"

Smiling himself, Will went abovestairs to his rooms and found he could hardly sleep. His mind raced with the coming audience, of course. Yet it was what he and Brianna had shared in the parlor that was paramount in his consciousness. Their passion play was delightful to be sure, but the compassionate way in which she accepted the admission of what had happened last Season assured him that she was the one for him. He had felt shame in the telling, of course. But it was readily eased by her sweet care and affection. He caught the indignation within her as well and knew that her heart also came swiftly to his defense.

"Remarkable girl," he said aloud.

He must have dozed off at last, for the next thing he knew he was being awakened by his valet.

"Good morning, Lord Shaston."

Will sat up and rubbed a hand over his face. The light was soft through the window so he supposed it must be early. He arched a brow and Cates smiled.

"Carson insisted we get you ready first thing," he said.

The truth of it struck him and Will quickly arose. "Then let us do so," he agreed.

After seeing to his morning needs and washing up, Will dressed in a snowy white shirt with a dark blue waistcoat. He shrugged into a light gray jacket and held himself still as his valet tied his cravat just so.

Dipping his head in thanks, he went belowstairs and found Carson waiting within the breakfast room.

"Your coffee, my lord."

Will drank it down quickly and thought for a moment. "Do you believe I should send a note before coming round?"

"Do you doubt your admittance?"

Will laughed. "No, but I do not wish to leave anything to chance."

"Then go to it, my lord." Carson waved him toward his study. "Make haste!"

Will dashed off a note to be delivered to Lord Lacey and waited a mere five minutes before following it in his carriage. He took the curricle again, eager to take Brianna into the park after his meeting with her brother-in-law.

When he arrived, he was not surprised that the front door was pulled open almost before he stepped down onto the walk.

"Do come in, Lord Shaston!" the countess said.

"Lady Lacey, how lovely you look this morning."

She dimpled up at him and shook her head. "Lord Lacey is awaiting you in his study."

"Already?"

"We scarcely received your note when he set down his cup and withdrew from the breakfast room."

Will's belly trembled a bit. "I did not mean to cause any upset."

She waved a hand. "No upset, truly. Just please go before Brianna loses any pretense of patiently waiting to be called down. Our aunt is no doubt at sixes and sevens."

He chuckled and bowed his head before letting her lead him to the earl's study.

"Come in, Shaston," Lord Lacey called.

"I shall leave you here." Lady Lacey seemed as though she wanted to stay, but she let him enter alone. "Perhaps you will take breakfast with us later?"

"That would be lovely, thank you." He entered the study and the countess closed the door at his back. He dipped his head to Lord Lacey. "Good morning."

"Good morning." Lacey waved him to sit and did so behind his desk. "I received your note. You wish to ask for Brianna's hand."

The back of his neck grew hot. "I do."

Lacey rested his hands on the desk and leaned forward. "I have no real objection."

"Real objection?" There was something in his tone that caught Will's attention. "Then you do have one?"

Lacey appeared uncomfortable, but in Will's memory that was not an unusual state for him. Before marrying his countess, that was.

"I heard of something untoward about you last Season,

Shaston. Something regarding a certain widow of some social standing."

Will's stomach churned. The gentleman clearly spoke of Lady Lasking.

"What have you heard?" he had to know.

"Just that you might have been involved in a liaison."

"I admit there was something to the rumors, but there was no affair."

Lacey's eyes narrowed. "And there is nothing between the two of you presently?"

"No. Never again." He took a breath. "If I may speak plainly, it is the reason I left Town early last Season."

Lacey nodded and held up his hands. "Then I do not need to hear anything more of it."

"Then, you give me your blessing?"

Lacey smiled then, appearing almost as relieved as Will felt. "I do." He came to his feet. "I daresay I would be unable to face my wife or her aunt if I refused, let alone my dear sister."

Will stood and held out his hand. "Thank you,

Lacey."

Lord Lacey shook his offered hand. "Welcome to the family."

A chorus of squeals came from just outside the closed door and Lacey rolled his eyes good naturedly. The earl opened the door and Will smiled at the three women standing in the hallway. The ladies' aunt, Mrs. Filbrick he remembered, clasped her hands where she stood beside Brianna. For her part, the anticipation on Brianna's face this morning pleased him nearly as much as she herself had done last evening.

"Mrs. Filbrick," Will said with a bow of his head. "Miss Brianna."

"You are to be mine, Will?" She colored slightly and giggled. "Lord Shaston?"

"If you will have me."

She nearly threw herself at him, only stopping at the last moment to grab on to his arm. "Let us go eat breakfast then. For I long for a ride in the park this morning."

Will bowed deeply now. "My lady's word is my command."

"That is a wise bet," Lord Lacey added.

After sitting down to breakfast with the earl, the

countess, Brianna, and Brianna's aunt, Will felt as though he had passed muster. The formidable older woman regarded him closely over her teacup.

"I believe you were in the group of gentlemen who courted my girls two years past," she said.

Will nodded. "Yes, Mrs. Filbrick. I was."

"And you waited until this Season to attempt to capture our Brianna's heart?"

He nodded. "I daresay I was too young to truly grasp the treasure Brianna is."

The woman raised her brows and nodded. "Very good."

"Yes, Shaston." The earl chuckled. "Excellent answer."

The countess laughed as well, but it was the expression on Brianna's face that made Will's stomach tightened. She appeared quite pleased with her choice of betrothed and, if they had not been surrounded by her family, he would have grabbed her and kissed her smiling mouth until she was sighing with pleasure. That, of course, brought memories of last evening rushing back to him. Forcing his attention back to his cup of coffee, he hid his own smile.

Chapter 8

Not long after breakfast, Brianna went abovestairs to retrieve her favorite bonnet for her first ride with her new betrothed. She could scarcely believe he had actually come to her brother-in-law and asked formally for her hand. Her sister and aunt had laughed and cried when she had told them of his plans. It had taken quite a bit of control to keep from laughing herself when her aunt questioned Will in the breakfast room. And when his gaze had settled on her? Oh, she longed to jump across the table and right into his lap!

As she descended the stairs, she saw that Will awaited her in the entry. Had it only been yesterday that he had come to take her for a ride in the park?

"Astounding," he said aloud.

He seemed to be looking at the floral arrangements coloring the space. She could see that there were new bouquets present since yesterday morning. He thumbed through the arrangements and withdrew the cards.

"Lord Wilbrey." He laughed. "And a bouquet from Stinking Stilling."

She covered her mouth as she giggled before

joining him.

"Yes, he sends flowers almost every morning," she said.

He turned to face her. "There you are."

The sound of his voice told her he was delighted to see her. She was certainly thrilled to see him again.

She held her arms out. "Yes, here I am."

Coming closer to her, he leaned down to whisper in her ear. "Something has occurred to me, Bree."

She swallowed thickly. "What is that?"

"I have not kissed you since gaining your family's approval."

Her cheeks flamed, and then she swiftly grabbed onto his shoulders and pressed her mouth against his. He froze for a moment before clutching her to him and twirling her in his arms. She broke off the kiss and tipped her head back, laughing gaily.

"You will be mine, love," he said, dropping a quick kiss on her lips.

"And you will be mine, Will," she sighed.

He set her down and waved a hand about the entry. "What shall we do about your lovesick swains, Bree?"

She placed her hands on her hips. "I suppose I shall have

to accustom myself to receiving far fewer flowers going forward."

"As they will be coming from your intended, I daresay you will have to make do."

His gaze settled on an arrangement somewhere behind her. She saw it then. Another bouquet of red roses from her mystery suitor.

"I take it these are new this morning?"

"I am not certain." Her brows drew together. "Why has he not made his identity known?"

Will frowned slightly. "I repeat, it is not very gentlemanly. And to send roses to my betrothed."

She laughed at his teasing. "I am only very recently your betrothed, Will."

He grinned and held out his elbow. "The park awaits, Bree."

Oh, she did so love it when he called her by her nickname. Out on the walk he assisted her up into his curricle again. As he piloted it through the traffic on the way to the park, her mind raced with all of the preparations necessary for their wedding. Something occurred to her.

"When will we marry, Will?"

"As soon as it can be arranged. I'll speak with my man of business and set things in motion."

She held on to his arm with both hands and leaned toward him. "When will I meet your family?"

He stiffened for a brief moment, and then nodded. "I will write my mother and sister today and make the arrangements for us to head into Essex. I think you will like Shaston Court."

"I am certain I will."

Her mind raced with questions about his mother and his sister, about his country estate, but they soon entered the park. They were fairly swamped with friends and acquaintances, and she attempted to keep up with all that was going on around her. Will appeared quite pleased with the attention, and proud to present her as his bride-to-be.

She smiled and nodded, but her senses were seriously overwhelmed. All and sundry appeared surprised by the announcement of their engagement, and more than one gentleman seemed like they had their noses tweaked. Will seemed to take it all in his stride, but she could not help but feel uncomfortable as the center of attention. That was passing strange, as she had never been particularly shy, and no one would ever have called her a wallflower since coming to Town.

"Will," she said softly.

There seemed to be so many conversations going on around them, but he must have been in tune with her as he stopped and faced her.

"What is it?"

"Is there a place that is bit quieter than this particular track?"

He smiled and nodded. "I bow to my lady's wishes."

His lady! Oh, if they did not leave the park very soon, she would soon shock everyone by throwing her arms around his neck and begging him to kiss her.

"I regret that we must cut this visit short," he announced. "My betrothed and I have another engagement this morning."

The people around them began to protest but there was no getting in the way of Will's fine carriage. As they pulled away from the crowds, Brianna breathed a sigh of relief.

"Thank you," she said.

Will nodded. "I meant what I said, Bree. I bow to your wishes."

She reached out and placed her hand on his muscled thigh. "All of my wishes?"

He laughed low in his throat as he shook his head. "You, my lady, will put me in a very uncomfortable position if you continue so."

She was tempted to stroke him, but she was woefully innocent in these matters despite their very heated interlude in his parlor.

"Very well." She allowed herself one brief pat to his thigh before removing her hand. "Where shall we go, Will?"

He piloted the curricle to a private stretch of track she had never been before. The trees grew thickly here, with cool dappled shade coloring the grass and the path.

"Will, this is lovely."

"Yes, but I regret I brought us this way, Bree."

"Why?"

He pulled on the reins and the carriage gently came to a standstill. "It is far too tempting with you so close."

Her heart swelled. "Truly?"

He turned and wrapped his arms around her waist.

"Indeed."

She could smell him again, and feel the warmth of his hands on her back as he pulled her closer. He kissed her then, at first softly and then with growing ardor. Her body trembled as he trailed kisses along her throat until he pushed aside the fichu covering her décolletage and stroked between her breasts with his tongue.

As he began to ease her bodice down, noises broke through to her. He lifted his head with a curse, and then laughed softly.

"This is not the most private of spots after all, I daresay."

She nodded and covered her bare bosom with one hand. Looking around, she could not locate her fichu.

"Bree?"

She looked at him and found him smiling as he held up the lacy bit of fabric. He held it to his face and breathed in before handing it to her. Her cheeks warmed as she tucked the fabric back into place.

"Quite a lot of modesty for such a small piece of lace," he teased.

She clicked her tongue at him. "Now, where shall

we go?"

He brightened. "What do you say to taking luncheon at my townhouse?"

"Luncheon?"

"On my honor."

She laughed. "That is a shame."

He kissed her again and flicked the reins, and they were soon on their way to his townhouse.

***

Will and Brianna were tangled together in his parlor again, and he could not be more pleased with that fact. Their kisses in the park were tame compared to what they were doing at the moment.

"Will," she softly pleaded.

He gently teethed one nipple while pinching the other. Her flesh was warm and smooth, and her floral scent was strong as he moved his other hand unerringly toward her center.

"I am going to bring you to pleasure, love," he murmured.

He dragged his tongue to her other nipple as he slipped his fingers inside her. She gasped and arched prettily beneath him and he could not wait a moment longer.

"I have to taste you, Bree." He kissed her and then flipped her skirts up and out of the way. "Please say I can taste you."

She bit her lower lip and nodded. "Oh, yes!"

He nearly shouted with delight before bringing his mouth to her pussy. She was sweeter here, slick and wet from just his fingers' attention. Bracing his hands on her smooth thighs, he licked and sucked until she was writhing with unspent passion. Giving her the rough side of his tongue, he stroked and stroked until she came hard and fast against his mouth.

He gentled then, licking her lightly as she let out the sweetest sigh. The sound, coupled with the sweet and salty taste of her, caused him to harden almost painfully.

"Oh, Will."

He looked up to find her flushed and pretty. "I wish I could take you right now."

"Please take me," she whispered.

His cock surged, and he knew he could drive into her and find blessed release. His desire for her was far from what he had experienced last summer. This was pure and sweet and hot, and he longed to learn how much they could be to each other.

Reaching between them, he began to unbutton his breeches. For a moment suspended in time, he held himself. A war raged within him. She was his betrothed, after all. She was here with him and more than willing. However, she was overwhelmed by her own passions, and he could not take advantage of the moment.

"I cannot," he rasped.

He shifted and sat back on the settee, his thighs spread as his shaft throbbed. The sight of her wet center nearly drove him over the edge, so he covered her thighs with her skirts once again.

"You kissed me…there, Will," she said softly.

He groaned and closed his eyes as the very recent memory played through his mind. "I did, and it was sublime."

"You gave me pleasure."

He nodded and grunted his agreement. Suddenly her hand closed over his cock and she began to stroke him as she had before.

"God, Bree." He leaned his head back and gave her free rein. "That feels so good."

"You need release, Will."

He nodded again and her mouth closed over him.

"Bree!"

She made a sound of delight as she licked along his length. Opening his eyes, he could only watch as she drove him closer to climax. He had been serviced in such a way before, but her unschooled ministrations were astounding. She appeared both innocent and enthusiastic, and he could scarcely believe what was happening.

He gripped the cushioned seat beneath him and gave himself completely over to her. Then he came, fast like a sudden thunderstorm until he was replete. Guilt threatened at the edges of his mind as it cleared, and he faced her. Her eyes sparkled and she wore a smile.

"Bree, I did not need you to do that."

Her expression clouded. "Did you not enjoy it? Did I do something wrong?"

"God, no." He tucked himself back into his breeches and cupped her face. "You gave me pleasure this time, love. There is nothing wrong about what you did."

"Or what you did to me," she added with a nod.

He could not resist kissing her again. "I believe it is a very good thing that you agreed to marry me."

"Oh? How so?"

"You will make an honest man of me yet."

She caught something in his voice he had not thought to infer, and she sat beside him again. "You are an honest man, Will. And you are the man I choose to marry, not merely agree to marry."

Her words cut through any lingering doubts he might have had before this morning.

"Then I am truly the luckiest of men."

She gave him a cheeky grin this time. "Yes, you are."

Once they had arranged themselves once more, Will rang for tea.

"I am famished," he said with a wink.

"You ate at luncheon."

"I did, but my lovely betrothed has left me quite depleted."

A servant came in with tea and a plate of biscuits, but soon left them alone again. Will shut the door and joined her once more.

"You are depleted?" She shook her head at him. "I

cannot tell if you are in jest, Will. That is not the least bit gentlemanly."

"In what way?"

"You are teasing me, but I am very new to this. I cannot tell if you truly enjoyed what we shared."

"Enjoyed?" He laughed. "I have never enjoyed such an interlude in my adult life."

She clasped her hands together. "That makes me so happy. I enjoyed it very much myself."

He nibbled on a biscuit and thought to tease her just a little bit more. "I believe the horses in the mews could hear just how much you enjoyed it."

Her mouth dropped open and then she laughed. "You are teasing me again."

"Guilty."

She poured the tea for each of them and sipped delicately from her cup.

"This is very new for me too, you know," he said.

"What is?"

"Having a woman here with me in my home. Making love to her and then sharing tea and biscuits. Is it not novel to you?"

She shrugged. "I suppose, but then you do not live with my sister and brother-in-law."

He nearly choked on his tea. "Do I want to know this?"

She waved a hand and took a biscuit. "Oh, I believe they consider themselves circumspect. But I have had to dash away from a closed door once or twice since they married. And not just their chambers!"

He schooled his expression. "I am sure they appreciate that, and believe you are unaware of…certain goings-on."

"Yes." She smiled. "Will it not be lovely to avoid such embarrassment when we live here together?"

Something she had said at that very first society party came back to him.

"Is this why you believe yourself a burden?" he asked.

"No, not truly. They have only ever treated me as dearest family."

He reached across the small table and took her hand in his. "You will be my dearest family, Bree."

Delight colored her features as she dipped her head and sipped at her teacup again.

"I should see you home soon, I think," he said.

"Yes, I would not want Marcus to call you out."

He feigned fright. "Pray, do not let him ever learn of the liberties I have taken with your fair person."

"He will not hear of them from me." She grinned. "I have taken my own with you, after all."

Her words brought back the pleasure of her mouth on him, and he let out a low whistle.

"If you continue to speak so, I shall forget my promise."

"Your promise?"

"Love, I am trying to keep the promise to restrain myself where you are concerned."

She tilted a glance at him. "Perhaps it is up to me to urge you to break that silly promise."

He closed his eyes and said a silent prayer as she laughed gaily. This woman was going to be the death of him, and would he not enjoy himself on the way to that eternal reward?

After tea was finished and he had ferried her safely back to Lacey's townhouse, Will returned to find Carson in the entry.

"I take it Miss Brianna is safely home?" he asked.

"Trust me, Carson, I will make certain Miss

Brianna is safe wherever she may be."

"Very good, my lord."

Will hid his smile and went into his study to pen a letter to his mother. In the few weeks since returning to Town, the scant communication from the woman did little to encourage him that her moods had somehow lifted. Her very written words were flat and emotionless, as if she could scarcely rouse the energy to communicate with her only son.

With resignation, he withdrew a bit of foolscap and wrote to his mother informing her of his and Brianna's upcoming visit. He set their arrival for five days hence and, after setting it aside, he dashed off a note to Brianna.

He rang for Carson and nearly collided with the butler as he left his study.

"Yes, my lord?"

"Were you waiting here, Carson?"

Nothing seemed to change the expression of the unflappable servant. "Did you need something?"

He handed Carson the letter and the note. "Please post this letter to Shaston Court, and see this note delivered to the Earl of Lacey's townhouse."

"Will you be heading into Essex then, my lord?"

"I hope to, yes."

"Very good."

Will sat behind his desk once more, his mind on the coming evening. There would be no avoiding talk of their engagement at the round of parties but, instead of dreading it, he much anticipated going public with his connection to Brianna. She was everything he could have imagined and more, given that she seemed to be quite enamored of his fine self. He smiled.

He never would have dared to imagine that this Season would be so different from last. Elise Lasking had done her level best to tear down any confidence or pride within him. Completely cutting off contact had been his only recourse and, while he had missed his friends' company for the remainder of the Season, he had not and still did not mourn the end of their distasteful entanglement. Brianna's acceptance of him and his suit went leagues toward restoring his mind and his soul.

He would simply ignore the niggling doubt that something this remarkable could ever last.

Chapter 9

"How long will the ride into Essex take?" Aunt Hattie asked.

"I believe Lord Shaston said that we will stop in Chelmsford on the way, Aunt. Perhaps traveling eight hours or so on each leg of the journey." Brianna turned her attention back to arranging her gowns for the trip. "I can scarcely believe I am going to meet his family!"

"It is as it should be, Bree," her sister added. "He is fairly well acquainted with yours, after all."

Brianna breathed in a calming breath. These past five days had seemed to fly since Will had confirmed their impending visit to Shaston Court. In that short time, she had vacillated between excitement and apprehension. "I do so hope they like me."

Both Aunt Hattie and Marianne wrapped their arms around her.

"They are going to love you," her sister said.

"And I shall be there to make certain that your reputation remains intact," her aunt said.

Brianna refrained from rolling her eyes. She had fantasized about the long carriage ride, in close quarters with her very handsome betrothed. She would dare anything to get him to drop his blasted honor and ravage her. Biting back a giggle, she schooled her expression and kept her head bent down toward the dresses.

"Will did not mention anything about parties or assemblies in Colchester," she remarked.

"I imagine all of Essex is quite dull this time of year," Marianne said.

Brianna shrugged. "No matter. He told me that we would not stay overlong."

"Truly? His mother and sister will let you two escape so quickly?" Marianne teased.

Brianna believed Will did not wish to spend too long at Shaston Court. He had told her of his mother's downcast moods since his father's passing, but she did not wish to betray such a confidence.

"They will urge us back to Town to enjoy the Season, I am quite sure," she said.

Marianne clasped her hands, an expression of delightful anticipation on her face. "Once you return, we can begin to plan the wedding celebration!"

"The banns have been read this past weekend,"

their aunt said. "It is only a matter of two more Sundays' postings to see matters set straight."

Brianna nodded. "Will informed me that the church in Colchester has done so as well."

"Are you certain he will not simply apply for a special license?" Marianne asked.

Brianna's stomach gave a little flip. "He did mention he may do so when we arrive back in Town."

"Then you may marry as soon as it can be arranged!" Marianne said.

"It cannot be too soon," Brianna admitted.

"Truly, Brianna?" Aunt Hattie narrowed her eyes. "May I inquire as to why you are in such a hurry?"

Brianna's mouth dropped open and her cheeks flamed. Luckily, her sister stepped in with a laugh.

"Oh, Aunt! Not everyone is in the particular type of hurry Lord Lacey and I found ourselves."

Brianna knew they had been together many times before they wed, but that was yet another matter best left undiscussed. Even their aunt smiled at Marianne's statement.

"As you say," Aunt Hattie allowed.

Once Brianna was fairly certain that she had packed

enough dresses for but a few days in Essex, she followed her sister and aunt belowstairs for luncheon. To her surprise and delight, Will stood waiting at the bottom of the staircase.

"Will!" Brianna gave herself a shake. "Lord Shaston."

He smiled and bowed to her and her relatives. "Good afternoon."

"Lord Shaston, we did not expect you," Marianne said.

Will blinked. "I received a note just this morning, inviting me to luncheon."

"That is on me, I am afraid," her brother-in-law Marcus said. "I thought we could discuss details before your trip into Essex rather than after."

"It would be my pleasure," Will said.

Oh, would they agree to have the wedding sooner? Brianna managed to keep her countenance as the others made their way to the dining room. Will held his arm out to her and she could not resist placing both hands around his bicep.

"You look lovely, Bree." His voice was low and

caused a delightful shiver to course through her. "I have missed you."

She wanted to remind him that just last evening they had once again left the parties early and ended up in each other's arms. The memory of the pleasure he had given her caused her to tremble anew. She had pleased him as well, with both her hands and her mouth. Oh, she was surely a wanton for wanting even more.

He chuckled and brought his lips to her ear. "You are blushing, bride."

"Bride," she breathed.

Will shook his head at her and came to a stop. "Bloody roses."

She looked about the entry and saw that yet another bouquet of red roses had arrived. In truth, she had precious little time to devote to the blooms over the past week.

"I do wish the gentleman would make his identity known," she mused aloud.

"Yes, if only to allow me to call him out."

She looked sharply up at him. "Will, you would not do such a thing!"

He cursed softly. "No, I would not. But only because it

153

would bring scandal to you, love."

"Yes. Marcus is vexed about those blasted roses as well."

"Good. I am glad to hear that he and I are of the same mind."

The subject of roses and mystery suitors was dropped as they passed a pleasant mealtime with her family.

Before he left, Will managed to somehow get her alone in the entry once again.

"Are you ready for our trip on the morrow?" he asked.

"Yes, all packed. I am looking forward to meeting your mother and sister."

Something flitted across his handsome face, an expression of unease. It was gone in an instant, however. He smiled again and pulled her close. "I do not know if I can bear being without you this evening."

She touched his face. "One must persevere."

He growled playfully at her and kissed her deeply. They were alone for the moment, though she suspected her family was aware of everything that was going on in this house. When he pulled away, he pressed his brow to hers.

"You are very special to me, Bree."

"That is a good thing, my groom."

He smiled again and stepped back from her. "Until tomorrow morning, then."

After he left, she stood in the entry, her arms wrapped around herself. Her intense attachment to Will had not been a complete surprise this Season, but the fact that he would be hers forever was something that astounded her even now.

"I can scarcely believe it," she murmured

"It is the truth, sister," Marianne teased.

Brianna blinked and found all three of them watching her with varying expressions of indulgence on their faces.

"I…" she began.

Her sister and aunt laughed while Marcus just gave his head a slow shake. Unable to resist, Brianna grinned at them and climbed the staircase to check her trunk and bags once again.

***

The ride into Essex did not take overlong. Will had made arrangements at the Inn at Chelmsford for himself and the two ladies for their overnight stop. On the ride, Brianna's aunt had occupied herself with some type of needlework while he and Brianna had talked about everything but the fact that they both sorely wished they were to stay in the same room. Will knew that would be beyond scandalous, damn it all.

Thus as a matter of course, they arrived at Shaston Court just past tea time the next day.

"Oh Will, the estate is beautiful!" Brianna said.

Will nodded as he eyed the grounds and façade, pleased that the work he had begun before leaving for Town had continued to completion. The grass was neatly trimmed, and the foliage was bright summer green. It was cooler here in Essex than London, but not by much. Still, he was pleased the home appeared much more cheerful than when he had left. He could only pray that the atmosphere within was likewise.

"I am glad you like it."

"Very beautiful, Lord Shaston," her aunt put in.

Will smiled. "Thank you, Mrs. Filbrick."

After the carriage rocked to a stop before the wide front steps, he alighted and assisted the two ladies down from it. They were greeted in the large foyer by Hynes, the family butler. He was much like Carson, in fact when Will was a boy he used to confuse them.

"Welcome back, my lord," Hynes said with a bow.

"Thank you, Hynes. May I introduce you to my betrothed, Miss Brianna Ellsworth and her aunt, Mrs. Filbrick."

"Lovely to meet you, ladies." He turned back to Will. "Lady Violet is awaiting you in the front parlor."

There was no mention of his mother, which caused a stab of pain. He brushed it away.

"Do see to our things, Hynes."

"Very good, my lord."

Will waved Brianna and her aunt toward the parlor and through the open doorway.

"Will!" Violet ran over and threw her arms around him. "I am so happy to see you!"

He held her close for a moment before releasing her, and then ran his eyes over her. She was much like him in coloring, with her dark hair upswept and curls brushing her cheeks. Her blue eyes danced with delight.

"You as well, Vi." He reached for Brianna's hand and tugged her closer. "This is Miss Brianna Ellsworth."

"Miss Brianna!" Violet squealed and grasped Brianna by both arms. "Oh, I cannot believe you are to be my sister!"

"It is a pleasure to meet you, Violet."

"Oh, call me Vi. Will does."

Brianna smiled. "Very well, Vi."

Will watched the two of them together. He had not seen Violet so animated in the long months he had spent here. Her delighted excitement filled him with hope.

"This is my aunt, Vi. Mrs. Filbrick."

Violet nodded a greeting. "Welcome, Mrs. Filbrick."

"The house is lovely," Brianna observed.

"Yes, but I have seen far too much of it this summer," Violet went on. "We must go shopping into the village." She laughed lightly. "Your aunt, too!"

"Thank you for my part of the invitation," Mrs. Filbrick said good-naturedly.

"We will not be here very long, I am afraid," Will told her.

Violet's mood dimmed a bit. "Oh. Then we must make the most of your visit. I told Hynes to order tea just as soon as you arrived."

"Thank you," Brianna said.

The four of them settled on the pair of settees flanking the fireplace. The women chatted about the weather or some such as Will ran his eyes over the interior of the large room. His success showed here as well, with fresh paint and trimmings. It had been an uphill battle the first year following his father's death, and his debts had been considerable. With grace and good fortune, Will had turned things around and had been able to see to the repairs the estate required.

He watched Brianna where she spoke animatedly with his sister and a sense of rightness seized him. She looked simply perfect sitting there. As she would soon be his countess, he considered that a very good thing.

"What are you smiling about, brother?" Violet asked with a cheeky grin.

"Just contemplating my future, Vi."

He caught Brianna's eye, and she blushed as he fully expected. She gave a slight shake of her head in obvious admonishment. Perhaps she would make him pay for his impertinence later. When the house was asleep.

Tea arrived, along with biscuits and small sandwiches.

"This looks lovely," Mrs. Filbrick said.

"It certainly does, and I am famished," Brianna said. "Your brother insisted we press on after a very early luncheon."

"Really, Will," Violet chided.

"I was eager to see you, dear sister."

Violet clearly did not believe him for a moment, but she gave a sharp nod. "As it should be."

He took a breath and broached the subject he and his sister had both clearly been avoiding. "Where is Mother?"

Violet's face fell. "She keeps to her room most days."

"Oh?" Mrs. Filbrick asked.

"She is often ill," Will rushed out.

Brianna apparently took her cue from him and stood to cross to the large windows along one side of the room.

"What a beautiful prospect! Aunt, you must see the grounds as they sweep toward the lake."

When her aunt joined her, Brianna beckoned her closer. "I do not believe that Lord Shaston often speaks of his mother."

"Far be it for me to press for familial details, after the ordeal we lived through," Aunt Hattie said softly.

As he watched, Brianna gaze softened. "And we are the stronger for it."

Though they spoke in low voices, Will heard enough of their exchange to count himself lucky to be marrying into such a caring family.

Violet looked from him to Brianna and back again, a thoughtful expression on her face. He was quite certain that she would pepper him with questions once the ladies were truly out of earshot.

After tea, Will had Hynes show Brianna and her aunt to chambers for their short stay. Violet, however, did not leave the parlor.

"Brother, you must explain something to me."

He longed to sprint from the room and up the grand staircase to hide in his own bedchamber, but he squared his shoulders and faced his sister.

"What is it that requires explanation?"

"How ever did you find yourself so fortunate as to secure that lady's heart?"

He blinked at her. "Her heart?"

Violet smirked. "She loves you, dolt."

"She loves me?"

"Are you simply going to parrot everything I say?"

Her demeanor reminded him of their mother before Father grew sick. He found he liked this outspoken version of Violet.

"Do you truly think she loves me, Vi?"

Violet stood and wrapped her arms around him once again. "How could she not?"

He dropped a kiss on her brow and the two of them sat together. Taking time to gather his courage, he poured another cup of tea.

"Vi, be truthful."

"About?"

"Mother."

His sister's expression soured. "She is barely here, Will. Oh, there are days when she is much like she had been."

"Only days?"

Violet nodded. "They do seem to happen more frequently of late."

"Then that is good news."

She shrugged. "I suppose."

"You did tell her of our visit, yes?"

"Yes, and she promised to be down for dinner."

The tightness in his chest eased a bit. "Very good."

Brianna and her aunt soon returned to the parlor. Brianna had done something to smooth her hair and dress, but he had found her just as pretty when she had been slightly rumpled from their carriage ride.

"Would you like a quick tour of the terrace and gardens?" he asked her.

"That would be lovely," Brianna answered.

Violet came to her feet. "And I shall show Mrs. Filbrick our library."

Brianna laughed. "You have found my aunt's weakness."

Mrs. Filbrick laughed and left the parlor with Violet. Will held his arm out to Brianna.

"Shall we?"

***

Brianna placed her hand on Will's arm, and they headed out toward the back of the great house. The doors were opened wide to the gray-stoned terrace, and the gardens were a perfect picture of lush greens, riotous blooms, and a cloudless blue sky.

"Your gardens are just lovely!"

"Thank you. It took some doing but our staff is very diligent."

"What do you mean?"

Will appeared troubled for a moment but then his expression cleared. "My father had not a real head for business in the years before he passed. I have been most fortunate in turning the estate around."

She nodded. As they strolled over the gravel walkways toward a fountain set in the center of the gardens she looked about, seeing little amiss. Perching on the edge, she waited for him to join her. He held his shoulders straight and appeared satisfied as he took in the details of the gardens and the back of the estate house.

"You are proud of Shaston Court," she said with a smile.

"I am." He studied the gravel beneath his feet. "I am sorry my mother did not greet you."

"There is no need for apologies. I am certain I shall meet your mother soon. Will she come to London for the wedding?"

"I do hope so. I think coming to Town with Violet would do her good."

"That is settled, then." She grinned. "I adore your sister, by the way."

He chuckled. "Violet is a force of nature, to be sure."

"She is nothing that I myself was not at her age."

He nodded. "She longs for a Season."

A wonderful notion occurred to her. "Then we shall host her in Town next Season, and she shall have it."

"You would do that?"

"She will be my sister, Will. It would be my privilege and my pleasure."

He drew her close and kissed her. "Thank you, Bree."

She cuddled closer and placed a hand on his chest between them. "I am glad you are no longer wearing that troubled expression."

"Did I appear troubled?"

She waved a hand. "Never mind. You are entitled to your moods."

His brows raised, and she knew he was sufficiently

diverted as she had planned. "My moods?"

"Brooding Will is intriguing, to be sure."

He scoffed. "I brood now, do I?"

"Yes." She touched a finger to the space between his brows. "Sometimes there is a little line right here."

He took her hand away from his face and kissed her knuckles. "I shall try my utmost to keep from brooding."

She gave him a look of triumph. "There is my gallant intended."

He just shook his head at her and held her close.

They sat for a while, talking about nothing of import and listening to the water bubbling in the fountain, until it was time to get ready for dinner. The rooms given to both her and Aunt Hattie were large and sumptuous, which brought to mind all he had said, and not said, about the condition of Shaston Court up until very recently. The ladies shared the maid sent to assist them and they soon found themselves belowstairs in the grand dining room. To her surprise and delight, Will's mother was present.

The lady was as gracious as could be, her still-pretty face alight as she gazed at her son. He had waited to escort Brianna into the dining room, and she felt his arm stiffen as they approached the older woman.

"Hello, Miss Ellsworth," she said with a smile.

"Lady Shaston, it is lovely to meet you," Brianna said.

"As it is to meet you, dear."

Both Violet and Will appeared uneasy but, as they all sat and talk began around the table, they both appeared to relax.

"Tell me, Lady Shaston," Aunt Hattie began. "Will you be in London for the wedding?"

"I shall endeavor to be," Will's mother said. "Have you settled on a date, William?"

"The banns have only been posted once," he answered.

"Banns?" She clicked her tongue. "Do obtain a special license, son. You do not want to wait, do you?"

"I do not," Brianna could not help but say.

The adults laughed lightly, and the mood was lifted a bit more.

"You have the right of it," Will said. "I shall write my man of business on the morrow."

Dinner continued as a matter of course, the five of them growing more comfortable with each other.

"Your sister is wed to the Earl of Lacey, is she not?" Lady Shaston asked.

"She is, yes."

"And you would be wed from his London home?"

"With a special license, I imagine," Will answered.

"Oh, yes!" Brianna said. "Marcus is to give me away in any event."

Her brows raised and, in that instance, she greatly resembled her son though with a more feminine air. "He is like a brother to you, I wager."

Brianna smiled. "He is, yes. He has been wonderful to our family and makes my sister very happy."

"Do they have any children?" Violet asked.

"A baby girl, yes."

"That is just lovely," Lady Shaston said, her face wreathed with a smile. "Will, you are marrying into a very warm family it would seem."

"I believe so, Mother."

"Count yourself fortunate."

Will caught Brianna's eye and gave her an intimate look that nearly curled her toes. Flushing, she dropped her gaze to the silverware in front of her.

"I do, indeed," Will said.

Talk continued but Brianna kept her face down. Her cheeks flamed anew as she recalled the heated glance Will had given her. Cheeky gentleman. Perhaps she would make him pay for causing such a reaction at the dining table.

After dinner, they retired to the library. This was another large and lovely room, and Brianna could not help but imagine spending many a cozy evening here during the winter months. She would miss her sister and aunt to be sure, not to mention Marcus and little Hannah, but to be with her handsome husband in wedded bliss here in Essex! That would surely be the most wonderful way to pass the time.

"Brianna, we must leave directly after breakfast on the morrow," Violet informed her. "Colchester is not quite the bustling city London is, but it has the nicest little shops."

Violet sniffed and shot a look of pique at her brother. "Not that I would know anything about London, Will."

Will rolled his eyes. "I know, Vi. Brianna was speaking about your upcoming Season just this afternoon."

Surprise rounded Violet's pretty blue eyes. "My Season? Oh!" She hugged Brianna and then Will. "I am sorry for every dark thought I ever had of you, Will."

He chuckled. "Dark thoughts, eh?"

Violet shrugged and turned to her mother. "Will you come with us to London next year, Mother?"

Something akin to fear crossed the older woman's face. "I do not believe so."

"You would be as welcome as Violet, Lady Shaston," Brianna said.

Her expression warmed considerably. "Then perhaps I shall attempt to do so, at least for a few weeks."

Violet clapped her hands. "I daresay I am happy you have chosen to wed this particular young woman, Will. She is simply perfect."

It was Brianna's turn to scoff. "I would not say I am perfect."

"Perfect for Will, then."

A glance at Will showed his warm interest in her, and Brianna grinned.

"That," she said, "I shall accept."

Chapter 10

Will sat in his study the next afternoon, pleased for the relative quiet. All of the women, except for his mother, had departed directly after breakfast. He could still picture the expression of delight on his little sister's face, and Brianna had been of a similar countenance.

He penned a letter to his man of business requesting he obtain a special license on his behalf and see it delivered to his London address. He then rang for Hynes to see it delivered directly. With any hope, he should be able to marry Brianna as soon as her family could make the arrangements. He would not crow too loudly over Brianna about the fact that all he had to do was merely show up.

Setting that pleasant matter aside, he perused his most recent estate records from his steward. He was pleased to see that his father's tenants—his tenants, he mentally corrected himself—appeared to continue their good fortunes. It had cost a bit to bring the farm buildings up to snuff but, working with them, he now shared a fair rapport with them. It was gratifying to know that he would be bringing his bride to a successful estate come the autumn.

A light tapping came at his door.

"Come in," he said.

To his astonishment, his mother opened the door.

"Mother?"

She held her hands tightly in front of her and her expression appeared tight.

"Hello, William."

He blinked, and then waved a hand. "Please sit, Mother."

She appeared to lose a bit of her stiffness as she did so. "I hope I am not keeping you from your work."

He closed the records book and set it aside. "You are not. I am happy to say that Shaston Court is doing well."

"That is good news, and due to your diligence."

He dipped his head in thanks. "Was there something you needed?"

She looked down at the hands clasped once again in her lap. "I just wanted to let you know how much I like your Brianna."

"Thank you, Mother. I like her very much."

She faced him again, now wearing a smile that looked more natural. "And she cares for you."

"That is a fine state of affairs, is it not?"

She laughed softly, and it struck him that the sound was the first such he had heard from her since his father fell ill.

"How are you, Mother?" he asked.

"I am well, as you see." Her brow furrowed and he was reminded of what Brianna had said of his personal brooding expression. "I admit I have been melancholy."

"I know, and it is all right."

"It is not." She straightened. "I have been a shadow, William. Barely here for your sister, as I had been when you were here last year."

"Mother, we all miss Father."

She sniffled. "Yes, he was a good man. Though not as gifted at business as you are."

The praise was late in coming but very welcome.

"Thank you for saying that."

"I am going to endeavor to be more a part of my children's lives."

He gaped in mock horror. "Ah, perhaps you should not say such to Violet."

She caught his jest and laughed again. "I mean to be involved, William. Not just with Violet when she goes to

Town next Season but with you and Brianna as you start your family."

"Family," he repeated. "Yes, I suppose we shall add to our legacy."

"And sooner rather than later, given the looks you two believe no one else has noticed."

The back of his neck felt hot at her words, but he managed to hold an even expression.

She waved a hand at him. "Do not worry so, son! It is good to desire the partner you wed. Your love will only grow stronger."

He had recognized the deep love his parents had shared and nodded.

"Love. Yes, I daresay it will be quite easy to fall in love with Brianna."

"The girl is nearly there already."

"Do you think so?"

"Have you never seen a young lady in love with you before?"

"No."

"But I believed you were doing the courtship dance for the last two Seasons at least."

"I was, but with no serious intentions."

"Until Miss Brianna Ellsworth?"

He smiled. "You are correct. Until Brianna, I had not thought much about love."

She came to her feet and, to his continued astonishment, came around the desk and wrapped her arms around him.

"I love you, William. And you deserve happiness in your marriage."

He patted her awkwardly on her back and she straightened. Her eyes glistened with tears and his own pricked as well.

"Thank you, Mother."

She dashed her hands over her cheeks and smiled once more.

"I shall leave you to your work, but only so that you can be free to enjoy the rest of the day with your intended."

He dipped his head again and she left his study. Her words and expressions appeared quite sincere and for the first time in a very long time he saw light at Shaston Court.

The bell rang for luncheon not long after, so he left his study for the dining room. As he neared, he could hear feminine voices in animated conversation. His sister's seemed to dominate but when he caught Brianna's his heart did a peculiar jump. It was passing strange, but perhaps it was due to all of the talk of love during that surprising conversation with his mother.

They ceased talking when he entered but only for a moment before taking up where they had seemingly left off. Violet went on about a certain dress she had bought and he attempted to follow what she was saying. His mother was also present, and she appeared to be enjoying the vibrant discourse. Brianna's eyes were bright, as she smiled and laughed and apparently tried her level best to keep up with his sister. His heart did that strange thing again.

When her gaze met his however, a different kind of light came into her eyes. Heat flicked over him, and he was grateful he was sitting. Were Brianna to continue to look at him in such a manner, his mother would be most assured that he was falling for his intended.

Hiding his smile, he bent to his meal and let the ladies talk over and around him.

"How did you find the village, Brianna?" he finally asked.

"Oh, it is simply lovely! Violet was right, of course. There are several wonderful shops."

He nodded. "I am glad you liked it."

"I pointed out the assembly hall, Will," his sister said. "They have several parties as the weather turns colder. First following the harvest and then for the holidays."

"I look forward to attending them with my husband," Brianna quipped, her eyes sparkling.

He stilled, and a sense of rightness added to the warmth he was already feeling. If he was not already in love with her, he knew he certainly toed very close to the line. He wanted to get her alone, however. To put the question to her and perhaps kiss her without any intrusions. A notion struck him then, a delicious idea of precisely where they could find solitude.

"Would you like to see the greenhouses, Brianna?" he asked.

"Oh!" She nodded enthusiastically. "I thought I glimpsed them at the edge of the gardens."

"You did."

"Then yes, I would enjoy that very much."

They left the house soon after, her hand placed delicately on his arm as they made their way. Once they were in the gardens however, she held on to him with both hands. Her side was pressed to his as they made their way along the gravel path to the main greenhouse.

"There should be no one working there at this time of year," he said. "The spring planting is complete."

"That is interesting."

He laughed. "Not particularly, but it does explain why I wanted to bring you there."

She bit her lower lip and nodded. "And why I want to go there with you."

He was pleased to find the place unoccupied as expected and, once they were both within, he secured the door. She arched a brow at him and he shrugged.

"Privacy," he said in answer to her unasked question.

The air was still within, and a touch humid. It was not unpleasant, though. He led her through the tables of plants in various stages of growth until they came to the attached orangery. The trees were thick here, and the smell of blossoms was thick in the air.

"So many orange blossoms!" she said.

"Seems fitting to be here with my betrothed, then."

She laughed. "Yes, we shall have to have your gardener send some to London for the wedding."

"That is a lovely idea."

There was a bench set off to one side of the space, and they sat very close to each other.

"Bree, I wanted to speak to you."

"Oh, that sounds very serious."

"Not serious, but it is important."

She gazed up at him and he could not resist her lips. He kissed her, stopping when she began to open her mouth to him.

"This must be important," she teased.

"Do you care for me?" he asked bluntly.

"Very much so," she said plainly.

"I care very much for you, too," he admitted.

She leaned forward and dropped a kiss on his mouth. "Then it is a very good thing we are getting married."

He kissed her, and then brought his lips to her throat. "Indeed."

"And by special license, apparently," she breathed.

"Posthaste," he agreed as he removed her fichu and kissed the fragrant skin of her bosom.

"Oh, Will." She stroked his hair and arched toward him. "That feels so good."

"God, yes." He tugged on her stays and one nipple peeped out for his attention. Closing his mouth over the bud, he gently suckled. "Sweet Bree."

She was pliant in his arms, her own wrapped around him as he teased and worshipped her. Shifting, he had her beneath him and he could not resist lifting the skirt of her pretty day dress and stroking her. As she had before, she responded lightning fast to his touch.

"Please," she whispered.

He did not need another word to give her what they both craved, so he knelt down before her and began to lick and tease her center. She climbed toward climax quickly, crying out his name as she came. His cock ached with want, but he sucked in a breath in hopes of cooling his ardor. He doubted it would work, but he sat beside her and closed his eyes.

"Take me, Will," she demanded softly.

He threw a look at her, seeing hot intent on her beautiful face.

"Bree, we cannot."

She nodded. "Yes, we can. We are to be married very soon. I want you inside me."

He gaped at her even as her words inflamed him more. "That is plain speaking."

Leaning closer, she kissed his neck and stroked him through his breeches. "You want me."

"Always."

She worked the buttons free and held him in her hands. "Then please take me."

This was decidedly different, her pushing for more intimacy while he was the one refusing. He braced for the oncoming regret he had known last year but it was not there. This was his Bree, sweet and innocent and desiring only him. There was nothing of this encounter that reminded him of that dark time.

"Yes," he capitulated. "God yes, Bree."

He moved and she was beneath him again. The seat of the bench was not very deep so one of her legs draped over the back of it. Damn, he could look at her all day in that position, hot and wet and craving only him. His body had other notions however, so he came up and kissed her as his fingers moved inside of her.

"I shall be gentle as I can be, love."

He stilled as his words struck him, but she did not seem to be aware of anything but the heat between them. When she was wet and as ready as he could make her, he braced himself and began to push into her. The proof of her virginity was there but he breached it. She cried out but before he could withdraw she wrapped her arms around his waist and urged him on.

She fit him perfectly, and he began to thrust. It was sublime, moving in rhythm with her. She was to be his bride, and the scent of her mixed with the orange blossoms was heady. It would be fast, but he was damned determined to make sure she came again before he did.

Stroking her little nub as he moved, he urged her higher. She began to cry out again, this time in obvious pleasure. When she reached the peak and tumbled over it, he gave up his own control and rode her until he found release deep inside of her.

Afterward, he managed to hold himself away from her. He was still inside, and rained kisses on her face, her throat.

"Bree." He had no other words. He had never felt anything like this before.

"Mmm," she answered.

For several more moments they held each other until he at last withdrew.

"Are you all right?" he asked.

She nodded as she readjusted her bodice. "It only hurt a very little bit, Will."

He cupped her cheek and kissed her again. "And it will not hurt again."

She gave him a sly look. "That is a good thing, because I plan to enjoy my husband quite often."

He chuckled as he tucked himself back into his breeches. "I daresay my wife may enjoy me any time she wishes."

She hugged him, murmuring love words in his ear as he let her affection wash over him.

"I am indeed most fortunate to have found such a sweet and loving woman. I will do my utmost to deserve you, Bree."

"It is not a matter of deserving." She kissed him again. "You have me, Will. And I have you."

***

Brianna held on to Will's arm as they made their way

183

back through the gardens. She had been afraid that he would refuse her there in the greenhouse. There had been an expression on his face, of acute worry. He had no need to worry where she was concerned. She had chosen him and wanted him beyond anything she had ever imagined. Not that she could have imagined much given her previously innocent state. A giggle bubbled out of her.

"What, pray, is so funny?" he asked with a frown on his face.

She stroked the line between his brows. "No brooding, Will. We are one now."

He beamed a smile. "We are, at that."

They spoke no more as they entered the great house.

"There you two are!" Violet gaped at them. "Is it so very humid in the greenhouse, then?"

"What do you mean?" Will asked her.

"Your hair is decidedly curly, brother."

He stroked his fingers through his hair and shrugged. "I believe it was hotter than we initially expected."

Brianna nodded. "Oh, yes. But the orangery is just lovely."

Violet appeared to accept their words at their face value and took herself back toward the parlor. When they were relatively alone, Will kissed her sweetly.

"You do appear a bit bedraggled, love."

She looked down at her rumpled dress and touched a hand to her hair. "I do, at that." She gazed back at him. "You called me that before, you know. More than once now."

He slowly nodded. "I did."

She could not keep from smiling. "I like it."

He took in a breath, in an attempt to control himself she assumed, and shook his head at her. "Go, Bree. I'll ring for a bath for you."

"That would be wonderful."

Feeling a bit sticky and uncomfortable now that she thought about it, she quickly kissed him and went abovestairs before she ran into someone else in this house. As she bathed, she thought back to all they had shared on that very small bench. He was a marvelous lover, and the tenderness in his words and expressions was even more gratifying than his passionate prowess. He had declared himself most fortunate, but she was more than likewise.

After her bath, she took her time readying for tea. A glance in the mirror atop the pretty vanity showed no outward change to her countenance but she had been changed profoundly. No wonder Marianne and Marcus were always wearing those expressions of fondness between each other. She herself would be hard-pressed to keep her new knowledge of passionate affection from the rest of those assembled in the parlor!

To her surprise, Will appeared completely composed when she saw him there. His eyes sparkled and she arched a brow at him.

"Brianna, you look lovely," Lady Shaston said.

Brianna had been surprised to see the woman in the parlor, but she appeared to be in better spirits then when she had seen her yesterday.

"Thank you, Lady Shaston. The maid you loaned us is a wonder."

"Yes, indeed," Aunt Hattie put in.

"It was my pleasure dear, but I daresay your appearance is not solely due to her attentions."

"Hardly," Will put in.

The three ladies eyed him, and he turned to study the view out the back windows.

"Hello!" Violet breezed into the room, her hands fluttering. "Forgive me if I am late."

"You are not," her mother answered.

Violet stilled and stared at her mother for a beat. "Mother, I am so glad you joined us this afternoon."

Brianna sensed a shift in the room, as if the melancholy that hung about was lessened still more. She could not be happier for Will and his sister. And for Lady Shaston, for that matter.

Tea was served and talk centered once again around the village and its varied shops. Before long, the conversation turned toward the wedding.

"I imagine Lord and Lady Lacey are in the throes of the wedding preparations?" Lady Shaston asked.

"When we left, we were unaware of the special license," Aunt Hattie said. "We may have to assist in the decorations and such."

Violet clasped her hands. "I would so love to lend a hand."

Brianna smiled at her. "And your assistance will be

much appreciated."

"Have you heard about the license?" Will's mother asked him.

After a heart-stopping look at Brianna, he smiled at his mother. "Yes, the license should be at the townhouse soon after we return."

"So soon?" Brianna asked.

"Too soon, bride?" Will teased.

Brianna held in a sharp retort, for she knew he was only attempting to get a reaction from her. As if he did not know he could all but rule her thoughts and emotions with barely a touch.

"Never, groom," she returned.

Lady Shaston chuckled, seemingly surprising both of her children. "I am glad you have chosen this young lady, William."

Will's eyes held those secrets again, and she imagined he was recalling everything they had shared in the orangery.

"As am I, Mother." He sipped his tea. "As am I."

Chapter 11

"By special license?" Lord Wilbrey scoffed and settled into the chair in front of Will's desk. "Remarkable."

Will leaned back and regarded his friend across from him. "Are you truly surprised, Evan?"

Evan shook his head. "No, not particularly. You are ensnared in the parson's trap as sure as if you jumped in with both feet."

Will could see his friend's point. That was certain. He himself could scarcely believe it was all happening so quickly but, after what he and Brianna had shared in the orangery, it was a very good thing to set a close date for their nuptials.

"I did jump most willingly, friend." Will chuckled. "And I would do so again, with such a prize."

Evan groused. "Ah, to hear a man spout such nonsense. It is sickening."

Will knew the man was only in jest. "Will you stand up with me?"

"What?" Evan straightened. "In Lacey's front parlor?"

Will smiled. "That is where the wedding will be held, yes."

"Then that is where I shall be at the appointed hour."

"Thank you, Evan."

Evan nodded and then his expression grew serious. "And how did you find Shaston Court?"

"It is doing quite well."

"All due to you, friend."

Will dipped his head in acknowledgement.

"And how are your mother and sister?"

"Violet is beside herself with excitement and, to my surprise, my mother is also looking forward to coming to Town for the wedding."

Will had no qualms about sharing this information, since Evan knew a bit of Will's mother's blue mood over the past two years.

"That is a very good thing, Will. Your bride is a treasure indeed, to bring about such a change."

"I should not be surprised, truly." He recalled all that he and Brianna had shared, both in clothes and out of them. "She is remarkable."

Evan apparently caught something in Will's tone, for his brows rose.

"Remarkable, Will? Have you and she…?"

Will narrowed his eyes. "Careful, friend."

Evan held up his hands. "I am not the gentleman to berate you for anticipating your wedding night."

Will chuckled. "It will have been less than a fortnight, Evan. That is not so large a misstep, is it?"

"It is not. Now you only have to hope that the wedding comes off as planned."

Will leaned forward. "We will be getting married. And in a very short time."

"I could not be happier for you, Will." Evan studied him for a moment. "While you were gone, the club was abuzz with your upcoming nuptials."

Will winced. "Should I be concerned over what was said about Brianna?"

Evan laughed. "Not at all! You should be more worried over what they said of you."

"What did they say, Evan?" Dread bit at him. "Did they speak of last summer?"

"No, no," Evan rushed out. "To my knowledge no one knows of your entanglement with that viper."

Relief nearly swamped him. "Thank God for that."

Evan waved a hand. "No, all and sundry are prodigiously envious of your good fortune."

"Let me hazard a guess. Bottom and Erlington have expressed their own thwarted plans to romance my bride?"

Evan laughed. "I would not press it that far, but they loudly lamented that another diamond is gone from the crown."

Will arched a brow. "There is a mixed metaphor in there somewhere."

"I am paraphrasing, but those two hens have been clucking."

"Any sign of the other? The man I tangled with at Joseph's and the pub?

"The prickly gentleman?" Evan shook his head. "No, there was no sign of him in the club."

"It is passing strange."

"You did not see him in Essex, did you?"

"No, nor did I expect to."

"Why are you giving this man so much of your worry, Will? He can be nothing to you."

"I suppose that is true."

"Then concern yourself with your nuptials."

"Very good advice, friend."

"Always." Evan folded his arms and sat back. "Now tell me about this astounding wedding?"

Will laughed. "I am afraid I know very little about it. I am to simply show up at the appointed time."

His friend came to his feet. "Then I believe we can manage to take a few minutes to visit the club this afternoon?"

Will joined him and they left together, bound for an afternoon of cards and conversation.

***

Brianna hummed to herself as she readied for her day. She was unsure if she would see Will today, as so much of her time would be taken up with wedding arrangements.

"Bree, do hurry!" her sister called from the corridor outside her bedchamber.

"Yes, yes." Her maid made some final tweaks to Brianna's hair and stepped back. "Thank you, Suzie."

Suzie smiled and dipped a curtsey before leaving. Brianna stood and took a breath, steeling herself for the coming activities. She stepped into the hallway and was surprised to find Marianne pacing there.

"Do come belowstairs, Bree. There are flowers to arrange and a dress fitting."

"Another one?"

"Of course. You are marrying an earl, dear." She grinned. "As I did, myself!"

Brianna shook her head as they walked down the staircase together. "Yes, I well remember."

"Now the ceremony itself will not be very large but at the party afterward there will be an absolute crowd."

"I wish the ceremony and all of it was over already."

Marianne clicked her tongue. "You will not deprive me and Aunt Hattie, not to mention sweet Violet and Lady Shaston, of this celebration, sister."

"I see you make no mention of Marcus?"

Marianne laughed gaily. "Oh, Marcus is of a like mind to yours I believe. But that is neither here nor there, for this party will go forward as planned."

Brianna held up her hands. "I surrender into your care, Marianne."

As they came to the bottom of the staircase her eyes were drawn to the entryway. There were fewer flower arrangements since the announcement of her engagement to Will but that did not mean there were none.

"Flowers," she murmured.

Marianne nodded and led her from the foyer. "Yes, and your betrothed continues to send increasingly larger bouquets every morning."

Brianna grinned. "I do love that man."

Marianne stilled her with a hand on her arm.

"What is it?" Brianna asked.

"Do you, Bree? Do you love him?"

"I do."

Marianne let out a breath. "Oh, that is good."

"What did you think, Marianne? That I was marrying for my own comfort?"

Her sister's eyes rounded. "Never! I thought you might be hurrying because you had an interlude that precipitated such urgency."

Brianna put her hands on her hips. "I believe you are not the one to assume such things."

"I know, I know. I just want to make sure that you have not put yourself in such a vulnerable position."

Brianna leaned closer. "I may have done, but it is of no consequence."

"Oh, Bree."

"I love him, Marianne. I think I loved him from the first."

"That would explain why you never accepted any other suits over the past two seasons."

"Too true." She winked. "He is the only man I could see for some time."

Marianne embraced her tightly. "I am so happy, Bree." She sniffled and stepped back. "Let us hurry with this planning so we can get you wed."

Entering the front parlor, Brianna was met with their aunt and the modiste. Her wedding dress was a glorious confection of creamy satin and lace and was decorated with more pearl beads than she could count. It was no hardship to stand on the stool while she was pinned and prodded, as long as she could see in the cheval glass the bride she would show to Will.

Oh, what would he wear? Surely a morning coat of black with a snowy white shirt and cravat, accompanied by a handsome waistcoat done in satin, perhaps in a lovely blue to match his eyes. She could picture him, waiting for her to join him for the ceremony binding them forever. And after the wedding, a breakfast followed by her and Will's swift departure for Shaston Court. There would be a ball once they returned to Town after their honeymoon, but she was focused on the wedding and their wedding night.

Brianna would finally have him to herself, to share everything they could imagine. And certainly things she could not even imagine.

"You are decidedly vacant this morning, dear," Aunt Hattie said.

"That, dear aunt, is the expression a bride wears as she imagines her wedding day," Marianne put in. "Or her wedding night."

Their aunt laughed and then visibly sobered. "Really, Marianne! A lady should not speak of such."

The three of them shared an expression that spoke volumes of secrets shared and kept. Brianna simply met her aunt's gaze evenly and the tender emotion on the lady's face warmed her to her toes.

Focusing again, she awaited the last pin and permitted the modiste to remove the dress and carry it out of the room. Suzie appeared and helped Brianna back into her day gown before leaving her and her family alone.

"I am so fortunate to share this with the both of you," Brianna said.

"You deserve this and more," Aunt Hattie said.

"Indeed," Marianne added. "Now, let us talk about the flowers."

"Will said we would receive orange blossoms from Shaston Court," Brianna told them.

Marianne nodded. "Yes, I received confirmation of that, and they should arrive the afternoon before the ceremony on Monday."

"I can scarcely believe I am getting married in four days!"

"Believe it. Your intended has moved heaven and earth to make this happen."

"Yes, not even Lord Lacey showed as much urgency," their aunt teased.

"Now, Aunt. You know full well Marcus was in as much of a hurry as Brianna's dear Lord Shaston."

Brianna laughed.

Marianne waved the two of them out of the parlor. "Let us look at the flowers in the entryway to see if there is something else we might want for the ceremony. In addition to orange blossoms?"

The three of them perused the bouquets, coming first to the most recent from Will.

"I do like the irises," Brianna said. "I believe those were also in the very first arrangement he sent this Season."

"You would be the one to recall such," Marianne said. "What of white roses?"

"Always lovely," Aunt Hattie said. "But not red."

Brianna nodded as she crossed to another bouquet. These were the red roses she continued to receive despite her wedding announcement. There was a card within as usual, and she plucked it out and read it. There was no name of course, but there was writing. Her heart began to beat wildly. Written on the card were instructions for her to meet this mystery suitor in the mews behind the house tonight precisely at one o'clock in the morning. She was to tell no one, or certain unsavory secrets would come to light.

She swiftly tucked the card into her bodice. There was no flirting or playfulness on the part of the writer. Of that, she was certain. There was a palpable threat contained in the simple note, and she decided that she would see to this herself. Fear and anger warred within her. How dare the gentleman, if she could call him such, demand such attention? And of what secrets did he speak?

Scowling at the red roses, she fisted her hands at her sides. She was tempted to lift the vase and dash it on the marble floor beneath her slippers.

"Do not fret over those roses, Bree," her sister said from across the foyer.

"I agree, dear," Aunt Hattie added. "I am certain you will no longer be an object of that unknown and unwelcome gentleman once you are wed to Lord Shaston."

Brianna looked over at her beloved sister and aunt. Forcing an expression of ease on her features, she nodded. "I shall take your advice. These roses mean nothing to me."

"Then let us go into breakfast," Marianne said.

After breakfast, more details apparently required their attention. Guest lists, menu, musical selections. She attempted to focus on these items, but the card from the red roses seemed to prick at her from beneath her fichu. If she had been alone, she could have read it over again, perhaps more closely until some sort of message became clearer. To decipher the sender's words in some way so that she was less than terrified to meet him. Should she tell Will? No, she decided in the next instant. She had no notion of what secrets the foul man had alluded to, and she would not put more upon Will than he was already handling with his own wedding preparations.

"What do you think, Bree?" her sister asked.

Brianna blinked and studied her sister for a moment. "Forgive me, but I am afraid I was woolgathering."

It was Aunt Hattie's turn to click her tongue at her. "Brianna, you have every right to be overwhelmed."

"Truly you do," Marianne said. "Why do you not let our aunt and I work through these details?"

"Oh, that would be wonderful! After all, this celebration is to be held here in your home."

Marianne seemed to catch something in Brianna's words, for she stood and crossed over to her. Settling beside Brianna on the settee, she wrapped her arms around her.

"This is your home too, Bree. Marcus and I feel the same way about this."

Tears pricked at Brianna's eyes. She gave a shaky nod. "I know, and you have never made me feel anything less than welcome."

"Then no more talk about this being "our" home. It is as much yours and Aunt Hattie's as well."

Brianna's throat was tight, but she managed to smile at her sister. "Thank you, Marianne."

"I tell you, why do you not go abovestairs and take a rest?" Aunt Hattie said.

"Yes, do!" Marianne stood once more and tugged Brianna to her feet beside her. "Go and rest, Bree. Let us sort all of this out."

"I could not let you do all of this."

"Nonsense." Marianne all but pulled her toward the doorway. "Go upstairs, or even go out on the terrace. Some fresh air might do you good, I daresay."

Brianna looked in the direction of the back of the house, though she could not see it from her vantage point.

"I believe I shall," she answered.

"Good," her sister said. "Now go and we shall call for you only if we are in dire need of your opinion."

Brianna gave them both a genuine smile now. "I trust the two of you to make these decisions."

They watched her as she left the room. Once she was out of their sight, she hurried toward the back of the house and out onto the terrace. Standing near the railing, she stared unseeing at the gardens.

After making certain no one was about, she withdrew the card and read it again. There was nothing in it that she had not seen earlier, but she knew she could not tear it up and ignore it as she so longed to do. No. This was some sort of threat to her and her family. Of that, she was certain.

Tucking the card away once again, she looked out past the gardens toward the back gate of the property. The mews sat beyond, a place where Marcus's carriages and horses were kept. She supposed the unknown suitor was sharp in choosing such a late meeting time. There were sure to be no grooms or drivers about at that ungodly hour.

"Who are you?" she asked softly. "And what, pray, do you want of me?"

Shivering despite the warmth of the afternoon, she fled the terrace and hurried up to her bedchamber. For good or bad, she would know the answers to those questions before tonight was over.

Chapter 12

Will stood in the center of the crowd, surrounded by well-wishing ladies and gentlemen, as well as gentlemen with decidedly less enthusiasm for his upcoming nuptials.

"Oh, Lord Shaston!" one older woman cried. "We were ever so pleased to hear of your news."

The woman, a society matron he vaguely knew to be the mother of a gentleman on his own bridal hunt, was surely being truthful. With him gone from the Season's competition, her son had more of an open field.

"Thank you," he said with a nod of his head.

Talk continued thusly, as he listened absently and nodded. All the time he was searching the room for Brianna. He had every reason to expect her, both here and perhaps later at his town house. It had been three days since he'd had her alone, and it was beginning to wear on him. He had wanted her from the first, but this craving was something he had never imagined.

"Lord Shaston, I am so very happy for you and Brianna!" a feminine voice said to his right.

Turning with a smile fixed on his face, he found

Patrice Prestwick standing there with an expression of genuine happiness.

"Thank you, Miss Patrice. I am the most fortunate of men."

"Yes, you are," she answered with a laugh. "Brianna is the very best person I know."

"Then I daresay you believe I may trust her with my heart?"

"Your heart?" She grinned now. "Oh yes, she will take prodigious good care of your heart."

"Your heart," he heard the other young ladies repeat among sighs.

"Do you know when she is due to arrive?" Patrice asked him.

"No, I am afraid I do not."

The lady's brow puckered. "That is passing strange."

Will looked about again. "I am certain she will be along soon."

"Well, until then I shall stand as bodyguard."

He laughed and looked at her again. "I thank you for your assistance, but I believe I shall be quite all right."

"Perhaps, but still. Oh, here is Lord Wilbrey!"

Evan strode over to them, his usual jovial expression in full view. "Shaston. And the beautiful Miss Patrice Prestwick!"

Patrice blushed prettily at his practiced words, and Will took note of Evan's particular attentions to the young woman. As they began to converse, Will continued to run his gaze about the crowded ballroom. At last, he spotted her entering with her aunt in tow.

"Excuse me," he began.

"No, no!" Patrice said. "Lord Wilbrey and I shall accompany you as you collect your betrothed."

Evan looked startled but soon covered the reaction with his usual charm. "Capital idea, Miss Patrice."

He held out his arm to her and the lady took it, leaving Will to make his way along with them toward where Brianna and her aunt were just leaving their host's side.

"Brianna, we have been waiting for you," Patrice said.

"Yes, Shaston has been in high dudgeon this evening," Evan teased.

Brianna blinked, and then smiled at the two of

them. "I appreciate your keeping him company."

"Hello, love." Will did not care who saw them when he grasped her hand and brought it to his lips. "I have missed you."

He stared into her eyes and knew that he could not have left her with any question of his meaning. It was two-fold, of course. Her company in public and her affection in private.

"Will," she said on a breath.

He caught both Evan and Patrice eyeing them with obvious delight and felt his own cheeks heat.

"If you two are longing for a dance, do not let us keep you," Will suggested.

"No, thank you." Evan turned to Patrice and stared down into her eyes. "Although if Miss Patrice will allow it, I would claim the next two dances once we are finished with our duty here."

"As you wish," Will grumbled.

"What duty is this?" Brianna asked them.

"The hordes, Miss Brianna," Evan provided in answer. "It has been an absolute onslaught of both well-wishers and jealous gentlemen."

Brianna paled a bit as she audibly caught her breath.

"Jealous gentlemen?"

Evan blinked and shook his head. "Did I say something untoward? If so, please forgive me."

"He is teasing, Bree," Will said. "There have been nothing but kind comments regarding our upcoming nuptials."

"Yes, Lord Shaston is correct," Patrice said. "Even among the meddling mamas, my own included."

That brought the color back to Brianna's face.

"Oh, that is good to hear."

"Is something troubling you?" Will asked.

She opened her mouth but closed it with a snap. "No, everything is fine."

Something in her tone felt off as well. Unfortunately, even the presence of Evan and Patrice Prestwick did not prevent more ladies and gentlemen from chiming in on their wedding.

"I imagine the flowers will be breathtaking," one young lady said.

"Yes, Lord Shaston is providing orange blossoms from his estate in Essex," Brianna said.

The other lady swooned. "How romantic!"

Brianna held tight to his bicep and leaned against him. "Yes, it is."

"Invitations are much sought-after, I imagine," another woman put in.

It was an obvious attempt but, as the guest list was not in his hands, he did not comment.

The lady's words were brushed aside as more people approached.

"Well, well!" Bottom crowed. "The couple of the Season!"

"As they should be," Erlington put in.

"Gentlemen," Will said.

"We want to extend our most hearty congratulations to you, Shaston," Bottom said.

"And best wishes to the lovely Miss Brianna," Erlington added with a bow in Brianna's direction.

She thanked them both prettily and appeared to lose a bit of her unease. Will had never believed he could be grateful for these two hens clucking in their direction, but he was presently.

"If only there were another such diamond," Erlington went on. He swiftly turned to Patrice Prestwick. "Ah, Miss

Patrice! You are easily as beautiful as your friend and much less encumbered."

Patrice laughed and wrapped her hand around Evan's arm. He appeared surprised by it but Will guessed he would not put her off for a ransom.

"You gentlemen are so very charming this evening," she said.

"This evening, at least," Evan quipped.

Bottom bristled, but then laughed. "Our mothers have decided that gossiping about Shaston and Miss Brianna's wedding is far desirable than plotting and planning to find their own sons' brides."

Apparently, the gentlemen were both pleased that there was to be a wedding soon and that fact took the attention off of the two of them to settle down.

"We are most happy to provide you this respite," Will said.

Evan barked out a laugh and Will looked over at Brianna, expecting to see a smile on her face. Her features were drawn again as she looked about the ballroom.

"What is it?" he asked as the others began to talk

among themselves.

"Nothing, Will."

"Are you troubled about something?" Worry bit at him. "Is it the wedding, Bree?"

"No, the wedding is the bright spot of my life to this point."

"That is good to hear. I thought you might be regretting your quick acceptance."

That made her smile. "Was it quick? It cannot be too quick for me."

"Or me." He longed to drag her into the nearest alcove and kiss her soundly. "Something is troubling you."

Once again, she appeared to be on the cusp of revealing something when her expression shuttered anew. "Nothing is troubling me."

"No, I am not helping to choose the flowers," Patrice said to one lady before them. "You must ask Miss Brianna about those details."

"Will you have roses at your wedding, Miss Brianna?" the lady asked pointedly.

"Roses?" Brianna blinked. "Um, yes. White roses."

"Just lovely," the lady said.

Talk went on, about nothing consequential, but Will watched Brianna more than he paid attention to the conversation. Evan caught his eye once and, seeing Will's disquiet, apparently appointed himself the keeper of all things jovial and light. Patrice did likewise, and he was grateful that he and Brianna could count them as friends.

Thankfully, after sharing a meal in the supper room, Brianna seemed more herself. After leaving her with her aunt and Patrice Prestwick, he motioned for Wilbrey to follow him to the refreshments.

"What is it, Will?" Evan asked him.

"I am not quite sure. Surely you took note of Brianna's disquiet earlier this evening."

"I did, yes. Could she be nervous about the wedding?"

"I pray not."

Evan winked. "Perhaps she has come to her senses."

Will just leveled a look at him.

"All right, then. What do you think could be the problem?"

"She seemed to be watching every person who came to offer his well-wishes. No, she seemed to focus on the gentlemen rather than the ladies."

"To what end?"

"I cannot imagine, but she does appear worried." Something niggled at the back of his mind. It was quite similar to the way he felt the few times he had seen the prickly gentleman. "I do not know who she could be watching for."

"She is surely not involved with anyone else, Will. Her devotion is clear."

"I thank you for that." It was his turn to drag his gaze across the crowded party. "Something is troubling her."

Evan placed a hand on Will's arm, drawing his attention again. "She has nothing to worry about with you as her champion."

Will nodded as he spied Brianna coming his way. His every nerve went on alert.

"I am taking my aunt home, Will," she rushed out.

"Is she unwell?" Evan asked, beating Will to the question.

"No, thank goodness, she is simply tired." She waved a hand in front of her. "It must be all of the wedding planning."

Will held out his arm. "I shall call for Lacey's carriage."

"Oh, no. I have already instructed a servant to do so."

"If you are certain." He leaned close to her ear. "Will I see you…later?"

She shook her head. "In the morning. Do come for breakfast?"

"All right."

Will watched Brianna and her aunt make their way toward the entry.

"Something strange is going on," he said under his breath.

Evan heard him, of course. "I shall keep my eyes and ears open for any information that can be gleaned from the endless tide of gossip at these things."

"Thank you."

He nodded. "I believe I shall enlist the lovely Miss Patrice Prestwick for assistance."

Will nodded again. Something strange was indeed going on. He vowed to find out what was troubling Brianna, even if he had to wait until tomorrow morning to question her again.

***

Brianna shivered in the small, tufted chair beside the hearth in her bedchamber, her eyes on the clock resting on the mantle. It was nearly time to sneak out of the house and head toward the mews. She swallowed thickly. Will had been so attentive this evening, and she had very nearly shared all of this with him. However, in the end she could not. Instead, she had run like a coward from him. The memory of the hurt and confusion in his countenance still stung.

The identity of this mystery suitor was unknown to her, but the man seemed to know her. What lies would he tell Will were she to bring him along? His card had mentioned unsavory secrets, which could be her clandestine trips to Will's townhouse in the dead of night. Or perhaps he had somehow learned of all that she and Will had gotten up to in Essex.

Her aunt had expressed concern when she had asked to return home relatively early, but Brianna had alluded to fatigue due to the wedding plans. It was precisely what she had falsely attributed to her aunt's desire to leave the party, actually. She detested lying, unless it was to sneak off to

Will's townhouse. That first night now seemed like so long ago when it was just last month!

After readying for bed with the assistance of her maid, she then changed into a simple blue gown she could easily get into and out of by herself. In the hour or so since then, she had been sitting and waiting for the house to go to sleep.

When the clock read ten minutes to one, she draped a dark cloak over her arm and quietly left her bedchamber to head down the staircase. The town house was very still, and she held her breath as she crossed through the hall toward the doors to the balcony. Once outside, she donned the cloak and hurried through the gardens.

It was a cloudy night, so very little moonlight lit her path toward the mews. Her heart pounded as she took small steps toward the stables. When she was secreted behind the garden wall, she held her breath. Something caught her eye on the ground not far from her. It was a red rose, and in the gloom of the night the color was as dark as blood. She reached down and picked it up, and its sickeningly sweet scent wrapped around her.

"Dear Brianna," a masculine voice called softly.

The hairs on the back of her neck stood straight as her heart skipped a beat. She squared her shoulders in an attempt to gather her courage.

"I am here," she whispered.

A low laugh reached her ears. "Just as I instructed."

The unknown man's brazen words helped to steel her resolve.

"Show yourself," she commanded.

Movement to her right caught her eye and she watched as he stepped closer. Just then the clouds shifted, and she could see him clearly. The large dark-haired man was very familiar, and a more detestable person she had yet to meet. Recognition slammed through her and the rose fell from her hands as she stared at him in utter shock.

"John."

He smiled, a false expression on his somewhat handsome face. "It's a pleasure to see you, my dear cousin."

She shrank back against the wall. "What are you doing here?"

He shrugged and ambled closer. "Can't I come to visit

family?"

"I know what you did to Marianne, John."

"Do you?" He snorted. "She was a willing participant, no matter what she says of it now."

Brianna shook her head. "No! You forced her and we fled to London."

He ran a hand over his dark hair. "So you say." He looked back over her shoulder toward the town house. "Seems to me that I did her a favor."

She could say nothing to that. The memory of Marianne sharing all that she had endured was etched in her mind. Her sister had been ill-used and very nearly ruined. It was only due to Marcus's love for Marianne that they had all been saved.

"Yes," John continued. "Because of me she landed in the sweetest place she could. Married to the earl and such."

"What are you doing here?" she asked again, this time more deliberately.

"Millicent has died."

She shook her head at his swift change of topic. "Your wife."

"Yes, my dearly departed wife. She left me nothing, to my surprise."

"You married her for her money?"

"Why else?"

"She left you nothing?"

"Nothing of any real import. Seems she had a will drafted soon after we wed."

"She was smarter than you, I assume."

He scowled at her. "I had hoped we could at least live on her inheritance from her late mother, but then she got sick with a piddling cold and never recovered."

She could not recall much of Millicent, but the woman had to be clever if she had found a way to deny John in death.

She crossed her arms. "Tell me why you are here."

"I need money, Bree."

Anger flared within her. "Do not call me that."

He splayed a hand over his chest and his brown eyes widened. "Forgive me. Brianna."

"You received everything from our uncle when he passed away."

He nodded. "I did, but for reasons I cannot disclose I am unable to get my hands on the money."

"That appears to be your problem to solve."

"No, Brianna. It's our problem now."

She turned to go. "I do not have to stand here and listen to this."

In a shot, he reached out and grabbed onto her arm. "Yes, you do."

His fingers dug into her arm.

"Let me go or I shall scream the neighborhood down."

Cursing, he released her. "You love your sister, don't you?"

"Of course."

"What would happen if Society learned of precisely how she came to attach herself to the esteemed earl?"

"Do you wish me to go to Lord Lacey with this threat, John? Marcus would thrash you top to bottom."

"I don't want to fight. I want you to get me money."

"I have no access to any money."

He smiled then, a sly expression. "But you will soon, won't you?"

"I do not understand."

"You yourself are marrying a well-placed earl."

A chill washed over her. "I will not take money from him."

"Yes, you will. Once you are wed, you will do your best to get money from him." He laughed again. "Perhaps ask your sister for some tips on pleasing a man to the point of him throwing money at you."

She slapped his face. "Do not speak of Marianne so."

He rubbed his cheek. "I won't hit you back, Brianna. Not now, at least."

"Get away from here."

"You are protective of her, cousin. And your aunt, I presume?"

Tears stung at her eyes. "Aunt Hattie was your stepmother, John."

"Yes, and she was kind enough I suppose. What do you think she would do if she and your sister were thrown out of the good earl's extravagant home?"

She knew in her heart that Marcus would never do any such thing, but she would not point that out to John.

"I will hear no more of this," she said.

"Go, then." He held up one finger. "But hear this, at least. Once you're married to Shaston, I will call again."

With that, he left her alone. Tears spilled over her lashes as she hugged herself. What would she do about this? She could not go to Marianne or, heaven forbid, Marcus. As much as he deplored scandal, he would not hesitate to call John out and kill him on a field of honor. Duels were illegal, were they not? What would happen to Marianne and little Hannah if Marcus went to prison?

Shivering again, she made her way unseeing through the gardens until she was once more safely in her snug bedchamber. She dropped the cloak and stripped off her dress, woodenly donning her nightgown. Crawling into bed, she squeezed her eyes shut.

Every hateful word from John rang through her head. She had to do something to stop his threats, but what? She would never use Will so but, if she married him, John would come back with his demands. The answer came to her then. What she must do to protect the man she loved.

"I cannot marry Will."

Sobbing, she hugged the pillow and let the tears come.

Chapter 13

Will dressed with care the next morning. He planned to pay a call on his intended, after all. What had she been about last evening? Her mood had been odd, and several times he had noted worry etched on her beautiful face.

"I shall get to the bottom of this," he murmured.

"What is that, my lord?" his valet asked.

"Nothing, Cates."

After eating a quick breakfast, he wasted no time driving his curricle to Lacey's town house. He was greeted at the door and soon Lacey himself stood in the entryway.

"Good morning, Shaston," the earl said.

"Good morning to you, Lacey. Is Miss Brianna about?"

"She is in the breakfast room with the family."

When he said no more, Will felt the urge to fill in the empty spaces in the conversation. He did not at first, however. He did not want to worry Lacey over anything or cast any aspersions to Brianna's character.

"Is Mrs. Filbrick better this morning?"

Lacey frowned. "She is the picture of health. Why do you ask?"

"I was under the impression that she left the parties early last evening due to feeling ill."

"This is the first I am hearing of it."

Will puzzled over that.

"Really, Shaston. Something is troubling you."

"It is nothing, Lacey. I hope it is nothing, in any event."

The other man blinked at him and then chuckled. "It must be nerves over your coming nuptials."

"I do not believe so."

"Nonsense. Although I could scarcely wait to wed Marianne, I could not help but feel nervous as the date approached. Your wedding is in three days, after all."

Three days. He smiled. "Yes, that must be it."

Lacey studied him a bit longer and then nodded. "I shall let Brianna know that you are here."

"Thank you, Lacey."

The earl stepped off toward the breakfast room and Will studied the flowers decorating the foyer. Those he had sent were present, of course. He saw no sign of the damned red roses, though. He chose to take that as a positive sign.

"Will?" Brianna asked from behind him.

He turned with a smile, losing the expression when he read the worry clear on her face.

"What is wrong, Bree?"

She shook her head. "Nothing."

"Nonsense." He crossed to her and took both her hands in his. "Your hands are like ice."

She pulled out of his grasp and held her arms at her side. "I have to speak with you."

"Is this about the wedding?"

She nodded this time.

"All right, just tell me."

"Not here."

"Why ever not here?"

Her gaze fell to the floor and she nibbled on her lower lip. "This talk requires privacy."

He reached for her again and she stiffened. Holding his hands up, he acquiesced. "As you wish it, Bree. We can take a drive."

She looked longingly at the front door before shaking her head again. "The gardens."

With that, she turned and hurried toward the back

of the town house. Will followed, his gut churning. Something was very wrong indeed.

They gained the terrace, and she continued on down the stairs into the gardens. When she continued far into the hedges, he planted his feet.

"Bree, do stop and speak to me."

She hung her head and turned. Her expression struck him. Her chin quivered and her eyes were downcast again. "Over there, Will. On that bench."

He saw a bench tucked into a far corner of the gardens and headed there. She followed, her steps slow and plodding now. By the time she joined him, he was at sixes and sevens.

"Bree, what is going on?"

She sat and he did likewise. When his thigh brushed hers, she moved away from him.

"I cannot marry you."

Will gaped at her. He must have heard her incorrectly. "What?" he asked softly.

She faced him now, her chin lifted. "I cannot marry you."

"Why the devil would you say such a thing?"

"I have my reasons."

His head all but spun from her words but he pressed on. "We are to marry in three days, Bree. Three days!"

"I know, but it must not take place."

"You gave me your word, love."

She winced at his use of the endearment. Was that what was troubling her?

"Bree, you do know that I love you."

Her eyes rounded. "No, I did not." Her body rocked toward his for a moment before she straightened again. "It does not signify."

"The bloody hell it does not," he growled.

She closed her eyes and he saw tears on her dark lashes. "I cannot marry you."

"What is this really, Bree?" He took her hands above her protests and gently caressed them until she allowed this small contact. "Why do you believe you cannot marry me?"

Tears flowed freely down her cheeks now and he gathered her in his arms. When she came willingly, he counted that as a victory.

"Bree, tell me what is troubling you."

"I cannot tell you."

"Do you not care for me?"

"It is not that." She sniffled against his chest. "I love you, too."

His heart skipped at her words but there was still the matter of her very odd demeanor.

"Then why can you not marry me?"

She swallowed audibly and said nothing more.

"I love you and you love me," he stated, struggling to hold on to his control. "I have a special license, for God's sake."

She was quiet still.

"If those are not reason enough," he continued, "there is the fact that you and I have been intimate."

She gasped and lifted her head, her face pale. "Oh!"

He nodded slowly. "Even now, you could be carrying my child."

Slapping her hands over her face, she began to sob loudly. He was flummoxed. What the devil was wrong with her?

"Bree, I need to know that you will marry me."

Shaking her head, she cried brokenly. Gathering her in

his arms once more, he held her close and rubbed a hand over her back. After several moments, she at last straightened and gazed up at him.

"We must marry, then." Her voice was flat and her expression far from one of a blushing bride.

"That is not the bubbly bride I remembered from two days past, but I shall take you at your word."

She grabbed his hands now, her grip almost desperate. "I love you, Will." Her words came in a rush. "I promise I will never do anything to hurt you. Not ever."

He cupped her cheek and wiped away a tear on her cheek. "I know you, Bree. I know you would never hurt me."

"Three days." She sniffed again and nodded. "We will wed in three days."

Bringing his mouth to her trembling lips, he kissed her. To his surprise she returned the kiss with increasing ardor until they were panting in each other's arms.

"Will, I am so sorry," she breathed between kisses. "Please forgive me."

He moved his hands to her waist to pull her onto

his lap. "Will you tell me why you had decided you could not marry me, Bree?"

"No. I cannot."

He nuzzled the side of her neck. "But you will marry me?"

She gripped his shoulders and leaned her head back. "Yes."

Unable to resist, he tugged down the bodice of her dress and took one nipple in his mouth. She arched toward him and sighed his name. He slowly pulled up her skirts to bare one leg, teasing her breasts as he stroked her thigh. His body hardened and he craved her in an instant. Touching her flesh, he found her wet and eager as he roused her more fully.

"Bree," he murmured.

She reached between them and stroked him through his breeches. "Take me, Will."

His breath caught and he could only nod. He all but tore open his breeches, and then lifted her and in one motion brought her down on him. She cried out and he covered her mouth with his as they began to move together. It was fast and incredible, and they moved as one. Their pleasure seemed to go on forever even as they climbed higher and higher still. He caught her cries of completion as she shuddered against him, and he came soon after.

They sat on the bench, entwined as closely as they could be. He leaned back and she rested against his chest, her breaths easing at last.

"Bree," he said again.

She muttered something in answer, soft and sweet.

"We did it again," he pointed out.

She finally lifted her head to face him. "Is this why you followed me out here?"

He found a smile and shook his head. "It was never my intention to take you on yet another bench."

She laughed, sound light. "In three days, you may take me in a bed, I daresay."

He held her close and buried his face in her hair. "I do love you."

She was quiet for a beat and then nodded. "I shall try my best to be a good wife."

He wanted to drag the truth out of her. To learn what had caused her to want to cancel their wedding. Now, however? With her soft and sweet in his arms and the echoes of passion still flitting over his nerves, he could not bring himself to cause her more pain.

"I have no doubts on that count, love," he said.

That would not be the last of it, though. He would learn precisely what had made her so uneasy.

She would be his wife and he would protect her no matter what the trouble might be.

***

Bree readied for the coming evening's parties, her mind filled with all that had happened between her and Will that morning. After their horrid exchange in the gardens, brought about by her secret, and after their amazing lovemaking, brought about by her remarkable betrothed, she had declined to take him up on his offer of a ride through the park. It would surely be enough to face all and sundry at the parties. She had no desire to deal with all of the gossip traders in the park. She could have no notion as to whom John had already been telling his tales. She would find a way to silence him without involving Will or his money. If only Will had not convinced her to still marry him, not that she had truly required any sort of incentive save for his loving words and clever hands.

"I tried my best," she muttered.

"What is that, miss?" her maid asked.

"Nothing, Suzie. I was just thinking about the coming wedding."

Suzie smiled. "You are going to be a vision, miss. Your groom is scarcely going to be able to speak when he sees you."

Brianna waved a hand. "I will look no better or worse than any other bride on her wedding day."

"Perhaps, but you love your groom."

The girl's plain statement brought a smile to Brianna's face. "I do."

Suzie nodded. "Then you shall have happiness like Lord and Lady Lacey."

"That is my fondest hope, Suzie."

"You deserve every happiness, miss. You are the kindest lady I have ever served."

Brianna could only nod, her throat tight.

Once Suzie was finished with Brianna's hair, she left to see if Aunt Hattie was in need of anything. Brianna stared at herself in the mirror.

"Will loves me," she said. "And I love him."

That assurance filled her with warmth. What they had shared on that garden bench filled her with heat, but she could not think about that now. She had tried to break off the marriage to save everyone from John's horrid scheme. Now she would have to pay the piper, as it were, once she and Will were married.

She would not involve her sister or the earl, either. It would be too cruel to bring about anything to overshadow the love they shared. And what of little Hannah? That sweet baby girl deserved the happy home Marianne and Marcus had built for her. Brianna would simply have to discern a way to keep John away from the family.

She could not divulge the truth to Will. Marianne's secret was not hers to tell. Furthermore, she did not want Will anywhere near John or his poison.

Someone rapped on her door.

"Come in," she called.

"Are you ready?" Aunt Hattie said from the open doorway.

Brianna nodded and stood. "Let us go and have a pleasant time this evening."

Her aunt blinked. "Whyever would we not?"

Brianna dipped her head and gave her aunt a small smile. "Whyever indeed?"

The first party was quite crowded. Her aunt was soon seated with her contemporaries, leaving Brianna to seek out her own company. It was not very long before she saw Patrice Prestwick, however. The girl ran over to Brianna and grasped her hands in hers.

"I have been waiting for your arrival!" Patrice said.

"Why am I anticipated with such excitement?" Brianna teased.

"I want to hear all about the wedding plans." Patrice wound her arm through hers and tugged her along the perimeter of the ballroom. "Is your dress finished?"

"For the most part, yes."

Patrice giggled. "Is it as beautiful as can be?"

"I daresay it is nearly as beautiful as your sister Penelope's wedding dress."

"Hers was indeed quite lovely. Lord Devlin could not speak for three full minutes when he first saw her at their ceremony."

"What is it about rendering a groom speechless?" Brianna joked. "I suppose Lord Shaston shall swiftly follow suit."

"Where, precisely, is Lord Shaston following?" an arch, feminine voice asked from behind her.

Brianna turned to find Lady Lasking watching them. "Hello, Lady Lasking."

"We were speaking of Miss Brianna's coming nuptials," Patrice said.

The lady's face appeared pinched before a clearly false smile spread across her face. "Yes. To Lord Shaston."

Brianna caught something in the tone of her voice. "The wedding is in three days."

"You have my best wishes, I am sure." Lady Lasking's lips thinned. "Though I have serious doubts about your being very happy."

She left Brianna and Patrice staring after her.

"Hateful woman," Patrice grumbled.

Brianna watched the lady make her way through the partygoers. She appeared quite put out still, and the other young ladies swiftly moved away from her to give her a wide berth.

"Why would she say such a thing?" she asked Patrice.

"She is cruel. She has said horrid things to my sister Penelope."

Brianna nodded. "Yes, as she has to me and to Marianne."

"I believe she is jealous." Patrice lifted her chin. "It is sad, if you give it much thought."

"Jealous of whom?"

Patrice raised her brows. "Of you, Brianna! You are marrying one of the most eligible, not to mention handsome, gentlemen of the Season."

Brianna nodded absently. "Her comment seemed most pointed."

"Do not allow her to ruin your mood."

"My mood?" Brianna looked at her friend. If only Patrice knew all that was going on in her head at present regarding John's threats. "Do believe me, Lady Lasking's mean-spirited comments mean next to nothing to me or my mood."

Patrice studied her for a moment, and then smiled. "Good."

"What is good?" Lord Wilbrey asked as he joined them.

Patrice blushed at the blond gentleman. "Good evening," she rushed out.

"Miss Patrice, you look lovely," he said with a bow.

Patrice said something in answer, but Brianna was looking beyond Lord Wilbrey at Will. Lady Lasking was speaking to him. Her eyes flashed and her lip curled. When she touched Will's arm, there was no mistaking the anger on his face. He jerked his arm from her grasp and whatever he said next was met with a sour expression. She nodded and turned away from him and Will squared his shoulders. He caught Brianna's gaze then, and a smile spread over his handsome features as he made his way toward them.

"Good evening," he said.

She had not missed the meaning of their interaction, and her heart broke for him.

"It was her," Brianna said softly.

Will paled and glanced at Patrice and Lord Wilbrey. "May I have a word with my lovely bride?"

Lord Wilbrey and Patrice both nodded, and Will led Brianna toward the terrace.

"Yes," he said simply.

Anger filled her. "How dare she use another person so ill?"

"She does not signify."

"All must know of her perfidy, Will."

"No. I will not expose her, but not for her protection."

Realization dawned on her. "You are protecting your family."

"Yes, and you." He took her hands in his and brought them to his lips. "I would endure a dozen such uncomfortable encounters with that viper lest any of it touch you."

She could not help but be reminded of the threat John posed to their happiness, but if Will could face his demon, then she would find a way to take the teeth out of hers.

"Your courage amazes me," she told him.

"I am only brave when it comes to you."

"No." She smiled up at him. "You are brave to endure such, and brave to set it out of your mind."

He kissed her hands now. "Pray, let us not waste another moment of this evening on such a distasteful person."

"As you wish." She touched his cheek. "You have my word that no one shall ever hear of it from me."

He wore his relief. "I do so love you, Bree."

She longed to kiss him there on the terrace with the *ton* so close by. "And I love you."

He held out his arm. "Shall we return to our friends, then?"

"Yes, please."

As they returned to the ballroom, she vowed to set John and his threats from her mind and focus on what was before her. Good friends and great love.

Chapter 14

The morning of the wedding came at last, and Will climbed out of his bed before the sun rose. The other night at the parties had been a study in contrasts. First, his distasteful exchange with Elise Lasking followed by the sweet support of his beautiful Bree. It had nearly killed him to bring her back to Lacey's town house afterward, but he had to be strong. Soon, counted in hours actually, she would be his forever.

"Mine." He grinned. "Astounding."

He rang for his valet and Cates soon appeared.

"Good morning, my lord."

"Good morning, Cates. Today is my wedding day!"

"It is indeed, my lord."

"Then dress me like an eager groom so I can begin my new life."

Cates was clearly holding in a laugh, but he nodded sedately as he saw to Will's clothes and things.

Will donned black breeches and the whitest shirt he had ever owned and gazed into the cheval glass as the valet smoothed the fabric.

"The staff has made arrangements for Lady Shaston's things, my lord."

Will glanced at him. "My mother's things?"

"No, my lord. The new Lady Shaston."

"Yes. The new countess." Will laughed. "She will be staying in my chambers, Cates. Once we return from Shaston Court."

"Yes, my lord. Carson told us as much." Cates helped him into his black jacket. "Several trunks have arrived and have been seen to. Her lady's maid will be joining the staff."

Will looked about the room, taking note of a small vanity and another armoire added to his furnishings. "Very good."

"What say you, Cates?" He took a breath and ran his gaze over his reflection. "Am I ready? Do I make a fitting groom, do you think?"

Cates chuckled at last. "Very fitting, my lord. My heartiest congratulations."

Will grinned. "Thank you."

He went belowstairs and found Violet fairly bouncing on her toes at the bottom.

"Good morning, Vi."

"Oh, Will!" She hugged him and then brushed her hands over his shoulders. "You look even more handsome than usual."

Will scoffed. "What are you about?"

She wound her arm around his and pulled him toward the breakfast room. "Mother is awaiting us for breakfast."

"I believed we were to have breakfast at Lord Lacey's after the ceremony, Vi."

"Yes, but we must all have something to eat. According to Mother, that is."

Delight was clear on his sister's face, and he gave another prayer of thanks for his bride. This wedding seemed to be helping his mother come fully back to her family.

"Good morning, William," his mother said as he entered the breakfast room.

"Good morning," he returned as he served himself from the sideboard.

"Is this not exciting, Mother?" Violet asked.

"Eggs, Vi?" Will teased.

Violet rolled her eyes dramatically. "Your

wedding, Will. Today!"

"Yes, I am aware," he said.

Their mother smiled. Truly, she did appear much better than she had previously.

"Are you nervous, son?" she asked him.

"Do you know, I am not. I am marrying the sweetest, most beautiful woman I have ever met."

"She is, indeed," his mother agreed.

"She is perfect for you, Will," Violet said.

She is that. "I shall endeavor to deserve her."

He attempted to eat his breakfast but, as talk continued around the table, he began to feel nervous about the coming ceremony. Drinking his tea, he attempted to focus his mind on the party afterward. He smiled inwardly. And the wedding night after that.

"Are you two in agreement to staying here in Town?" Will asked his sister and mother.

"Yes, son." His mother arched her brows. "You and your bride may have Shaston Court all to yourselves, for a fortnight at least."

"It is so exciting!" Violet said. "Lady Lacey assured me that I may accompany them to any places open to me."

"Only a few, Violet," their mother said. "You are not out, after all."

Violet waved a hand. "Yes, yes. I know. I shall endeavor to maintain a certain air of mystery no matter where I go."

Will exchanged an expression of mock-worry with his mother, and the woman smiled.

He dipped his head. "Very good."

Thankfully, the three of them soon left for Lacey's townhouse. There were flowers everywhere he looked, including the Shaston Court orange blossoms they had arranged. Lacey himself met them in the entry.

"Hello, ladies," Lacey said with a bow before facing Will. "So you have come, Shaston."

Will laughed. "You could not keep me away."

He clasped Will on the shoulder. "That is what a loving brother likes to hear on his sister's wedding day."

After seeing Will and his family into the parlor, Will waited for what felt like eons for Brianna to appear.

"Shaston, you look positively pale," Lord Wilbrey said as he stepped up to his side.

"Do be quiet, Evan."

Evan barked out a laugh. "I am merely teasing you, friend. You do not have anything to fear." He shrugged. "At least, I do not believe you do."

"Thank you," Will said.

The rest of the family sat in their seats and the only ones missing to his eyes were Lacey and Brianna. When she stood in the doorway with her brother-in-law, after what felt like an hour at least, she took Will's breath.

She was a vision in satin and lace, and she would soon be all his. Her hair was upswept in braids and curls at her crown and was decorated with pearls and orange blossoms. In her hands she held white lilies and roses, along with more blossoms. Gliding toward him, she kept her gaze fixed on his face. Her cheeks were pink and her eyes bright, and her skin appeared as creamy as her gown. He had seen her in—and nearly out of—several different dresses but he was seized with the urge to fall to the floor before her and pledge his heart and soul to her happiness.

Once she stood before him, her hands now held in his, he was barely aware of the ceremony itself. He vowed to do whatever was asked of him, and answered in the affirmative when it was urged to do so. Staring into Brianna's beautiful blue eyes, he watched her rosy lips as she did likewise when required. They were married in what felt both like mere moments and endless hours. She dipped her face up toward him, beckoning him to kiss her, and he had to restrain from pulling her flush against him as he took her lips.

The two of them were soon surrounded by well-wishers. He held tight to her hand, and she pressed up against his side. Emotion nearly swamped him. He had never imagined getting married would feel so right.

"I love you, Bree," he whispered in her ear.

She squealed and wrapped both hands around his bicep. "I love you, Will!"

They went into the wedding breakfast in the formal dining room, and Will finally felt the stirrings of hunger.

"I could not eat a bite this morning," Brianna said.

"Neither could I," he admitted. "Are you hungry now?"

"I am famished," she said with a laugh.

He bent his head to her ear again. "I am as well, and not only for breakfast."

She turned to face him fully. "Tell me this is the

right thing, Will?"

There was a hint of trepidation in her countenance, but he would not hear of it. Not today. They were wed and he could not be more pleased that was so.

He cupped her face, his thumb stroking over her cheek. "This is very right, Bree."

Unable to resist, he kissed her again. They began to deepen the kiss when the sounds of their guests reached them. Flushing hot, he threw a sheepish look at Brianna and she blushed as well.

"Let us go in," Will said, holding out his arm.

She grabbed on again and they went in to greet their guests.

***

Brianna looked about the bed chamber she had occupied in Marcus's home for nearly the past two years, a twist of melancholy taking her. He was so good, taking in both her and Aunt Hattie after he wed Marianne.

"Are you all set, Bree?" Marianne asked from the doorway.

"Yes." Brianna's eyes filled with tears and she threw herself into her sister's arms. "Thank you so much,

Marianne."

"Oh, there." Her sister hugged her back fiercely and then released her. "You owe me no thanks. You are my sister and Marcus wanted to make a home for you."

"And he did." Brianna sniffled. "Now you have only Aunt Hattie to intrude on your privacy."

Marianne laughed as their aunt joined them.

"I intrude, do I?" Aunt Hattie asked.

"Never, Aunt." Marianne hugged her as well. "Pray, tell Bree that she will be missed?"

"She will indeed." Aunt Hattie placed her hand under Brianna's chin. "You deserve all of your happiness, dear child. It does my heart good to see both of my girls so happily settled."

Brianna nodded. "I do love Will so."

Their aunt put her hands on her hips. "That was quite evident at the ceremony."

"Truly." Marianne grinned. "I thought for a moment that Marcus would have to pry the two of you apart at the breakfast."

Brianna gazed at her beloved sister, her worry over John's threats never far from her mind. This was her wedding day. She would not poison the day with thoughts of that horrid man.

"That is as it should be, is it not?" she countered.

"Yes!" Marianne said. "Now let us get you ready for your carriage ride into Essex."

Brianna nearly trembled with excitement for the coming days spent with only Will for company. They would share even more than they already had, and she could not wait to indulge in every wild thought she had ever had with him.

"I daresay we need to get her belowstairs, Aunt," Marianne teased.

Brianna placed her hands over her flaming cheeks and then lifted her chin. "Never mind."

"Off with you," Aunt Hattie said.

She found her new husband waiting for her in the entry. He wore a bright smile and her heart flipped.

"Will," she breathed.

He bowed to her. "Let us be off, dear wife."

"Wife!" She giggled. "As you wish it, dear husband."

They said their goodbyes to Brianna's family and Will assisted her into his carriage. As it began to move, he held her close.

"I can scarcely believe we are here, love."

She touched his face. "We are, and you are stuck with me now."

He dropped a kiss on the tip of her nose. "Consider me a willing captive."

As they rode through Town, she could not help but peer out the window for any sign of John. It was only when they left Mayfair and headed east that she began to set him from her mind.

"As on our previous trip to Essex, love," Will began, holding her close. "We shall stop at that inn midway through."

She breathed in his scent and sighed. "Yes, but unlike that trip, I will have you all to myself."

He nuzzled the side of her neck. "To do with me what you will."

"Likewise."

Growling playfully, he pulled her onto his lap. "You made an honest man of me, Bree. You have my permission to do anything you wish with your lawful husband."

"It seems to me I did what I wished previously,

Will." She giggled. "On several benches, if I recall correctly."

He nibbled on her neck now. "I smell those orange blossoms tucked in your hair and think of that time in the orangery, love. When I made you mine."

"Mmm. I daresay I made *you* mine."

He laughed low in his throat, and her body tingled in response. "You were quite daring, as I recall."

"There is no telling what I might dare, husband."

He kissed her then, drugging kisses that set her on fire. When he reached beneath her skirts, she was just daring enough to let him have his way with her this time.

Later that evening, after sharing a lovely meal in their room at the inn, Will went down to the lounge while she got ready for bed. Her lady's maid Suzie had been given lodgings along with other travelers' servants, and Brianna had instructed her to take the evening off and only worry herself in the morning to assist Brianna with her dress. Brianna and she had selected her travel clothes that would be easy to remove by herself.

So Brianna ducked behind a privacy screen in the small but lovely room she shared with Will to change into her nightgown. It was truly no hardship for her, since there had been times before when both she and Marianne had to fend for themselves for the most part. She shivered as she undressed, stripped to her drawers, and slipped the nightgown over her head. The gossamer thin fabric settled over her skin, making her breasts tingle. To her astonishment, she was nervous about the coming wedding night. It seemed silly, as she and Will had already known each other more than once.

A knock came to the door before it was opened with a squeak.

"Bree?" she heard Will call softly.

She took a bracing breath and stepped out from behind the screen. "Here I am."

Will stared at her, heat in his gaze. "Lord, Bree." He shed his jacket and loosened his neckcloth, revealing his strong throat. "I cannot wait to feel you against me."

Stepping closer, she began to unbutton his waistcoat. "I want to see all of you, Will."

He dropped his hands to his sides. "Have your way with me, wife."

She bit her lower lip as she worked first his waistcoat and then his shirt off of him. He was beautifully made, sculpted and warm as she ran her hand over his chest and over his flat belly.

"I love how you feel, Will." She kissed one of his flat nipples and he sucked in a breath. "Is this not what you do to me?"

He growled again and closed his eyes. "I believe you will kill me before this night is over."

She brushed her palm over the bulge in the front of his breeches and felt him harden. "You want me."

"Always."

Abandoning her slow progress of getting him naked, she wrapped her arms around his neck and pressed her aching breasts against his bare chest. "Take me, Will."

He grabbed her in his arms and carried her over to the bed, and then set her down on the soft coverlet. His hands ran over her as he kissed her, leaving a trail of fire each place he touched her. Her nightgown was a memory as he covered her body with his. He was smooth and hard and hot against her hands as she ran them over him.

"Oh, my."

He closed his mouth over one of her nipples and she gasped. It was so much more than when he had kissed her there before. She could stretch out as she wished, throwing her arms over her head as he teethed her nipple. He trailed kisses over her belly and soon settled between her thighs. He had loved her like this before, but she was completely naked and felt no shame as his lips and tongue drove her higher and higher. He made the most delicious sounds as he gave her pleasure, and she soon crested on her orgasm.

"I love your taste, Bree." He came up and kissed her before resting his brow on hers. "And I love giving you pleasure."

His body stretched over hers and as he held her she could feel her passions rising again. He rubbed her center with his thigh, and her sensitized skin tingled.

"Take me, Will," she whispered.

He rubbed himself against her now, groaning softly. "I want to, but I was giving you a chance to collect yourself."

She placed her hands on the side of his face, looking deep into his eyes. "I do not wish to wait."

He grinned and shifted, driving into her in one thrust. It was incredible, the two of them stretched out and touching just about everywhere. He braced himself on his strong arms and moved faster. She held on to him, bowing back as she took everything from him. Her legs wrapped around his waist and every sensation multiplied.

"Will!" She cried out as her second orgasm took her. "Oh!"

"Christ, Bree." He moaned and his movements became less disciplined. "Ah, love."

His body arched and he held his big body still as he climaxed. A few moments later, he withdrew from her and fell to her side. Nuzzling against her neck, he let out a very satisfied-sounding breath.

"That was astounding," he murmured.

She purred in delight and cuddled closer. "You are astounding, husband."

"Mmm, wife."

"I daresay a bed is far preferrable to a bench," she said.

Laughing softly, he kissed her neck. "Then wait until you see our bed at Shaston Court."

She giggled, and then let out a yawn. He pulled the coverlet up over the two of them.

"Goodnight, love."

She echoed the sentiment and decided to put everything out of her mind but what she shared with her new husband.

John be damned. She would not let him intrude on their honeymoon.

Chapter 15

They arrived at Shaston Court the next afternoon and Will was soon pleased to find that his new wife enjoyed his attention as often as he wished. She very much enjoyed their very large bed as well.

A few days into their stay, they sat at the breakfast table in companionable silence. Brianna appeared a bit tired, but her cheeks blushed pink when he caught her eye.

"Are you enjoying our honeymoon, Bree?"

"Very."

Her eyes held a touch of heat and he counted himself a fortunate man.

"What do you wish to do today?" he asked.

She laughed lightly. "I daresay we should go into the village at some point."

"Why ever would we want to do that?' he teased.

Waving a hand at him, she took dainty bites of her eggs and ham. "I need to find some gifts for the family, Will."

He drank his tea. "Capital idea, love. You shall help me select something for my sister and mother, too."

"Gladly."

Within the hour, they were strolling the cobblestone

streets of Colchester. Will held boxes and bags of items but he bore the burden cheerfully.

"I believe you may have left one or two things in that last shop, Bree."

"Never mind." She wound her arm through his. "I simply had to have that sweet little jacket for Hannah."

"She is an infant."

"And?"

"Does she truly require a jacket of any kind?"

"You have clearly never been a young girl."

"Very true," he laughed.

"Ask Violet the next time you see her, then. Little girls need things that make them feel special. Besides that, she does not have a jacket in that particular shade of pink."

He shrugged, shifting the boxes in his arms. "I bow to your expertise in the matter. What say we go back to Shaston Court?"

"Very well. It is nearly luncheon."

When they neared the carriage, his driver took the boxes and bags and they climbed aboard. He watched her as she gazed out the window, caught by the very pleased expression on her beautiful face. She appeared quite happy with their honeymoon in general, and with her husband in particular. He could not help but think of that afternoon when she had attempted to cry off. His belly clenched at the memory of the anguish that had taken him then.

"Are you happy, Bree?"

"Hmm?" She faced him, gifting him with a bright smile. "Very."

"I know I said that we should never speak of it, but why did you wish to cancel our wedding?"

Her chin wobbled for a moment, and then she shook her head at him. "It was nothing, Will. I will never allow anything to tear us apart."

"Tear us apart? Did something happen to attempt to do so?"

"It is nothing I can speak of to you."

Unease struck him.

"It was not Lady Lasking?"

Her lips parted. "No, Will! She has never said anything about you to me."

He nodded. "Good. I do not want such an unsavory business to ever touch you."

Something flitted over her face, an expression of worry that was quickly gone. "We are married, Will. I am so happy to be your wife."

"As am I to be your husband."

She gazed out the window as the carriage made its way up the long drive to the manor house. He caught a glimpse of the gazebo set just beyond the gardens.

"I believe we have not yet made use of the bench out by the folly," he said.

She caught his eye then and her smile widened. "Is that so?"

"Perhaps we should pay a visit after luncheon?"

"I daresay that is a wonderful idea, Will."

They alighted the carriage in front of Shaston Court and Will waved her on ahead of him. "I have to see to something, Bree. Do go into the dining room and I will join you shortly."

She arched a brow. "What are you about?"

"Me?" He affected an expression of innocence. "Absolutely nothing untoward."

She laughed. "That is a shame, then."

"Go on, minx."

He spoke to Hynes about arranging a few things for Brianna and then joined her. Luncheon was light fare, mostly salads and such accompanied by crusty bread.

"Hello, love." He kissed her and took his seat beside her. "Sorry to keep you waiting."

"No matter. I have only just begun."

He began to eat, conscious of her watching him.

"Did you accomplish what you meant to, Will?"

"That, my dear wife, is a surprise."

"A surprise?" She clasped her hands. "Tell me! No wait, do not tell me."

"Just eat, Bree."

Near the end of the meal, he stood. "Are you ready for your surprise?"

She dabbed her lips with a napkin and stood. "I am."

He led her toward the back of the house and out onto the terrace.

"Will, what are you about?"

"I wanted to pay a visit to the folly, that is all."

She clicked her tongue but kept her hand firmly tucked into his bent arm. "Lead the way, I suppose."

They gained the gazebo, a lovely structure his father had

built years earlier. The columns were twined with ivy and moss colored the base. Inside were stone benches but so was the surprise he had arranged.

"Oh, this is so pretty!" she said.

"I always thought so. I made some changes for today, however."

She saw the cushions on the benches and a large blanket and pillows on the stone floor. A tray of sweets and fruits sat within, along with a bottle of lemonade.

"A picnic, Will!"

"A dessert picnic, love. Just a few things I managed to buy in the village while you were shopping. And the staff saw to the fruits and lemonade."

They settled on the blanket, and then she plucked a tiny cream puff from the serving platter and ate it in one bite. "Delicious!"

He watched as she licked the tip of her finger and heat surged to his cock. "You are tempting me, love."

Looking up at him, she dropped her hand to her lap. "Do you want some cream, Will?"

He growled at her and took her in his arms. "Pastries, later." He kissed her and pulled back to grin down at her. "Wife, now."

She moaned as he moved her skirts aside and buried his face between her legs. Gasping, she gave herself over to him as he feasted. She was surely sweeter than anything he had purchased in the village, and he took his fill. His body throbbed in near-pain as she crested on her climax. Before she could do more than catch her breath, he grasped her arms and pulled her up against him.

"I have to get inside of you, love."

"Yes," she sighed.

Turning her, he set her on her hands and knees.

"Will, what are you about?"

"You will enjoy this, Bree." He flicked her skirts out of the way and stroked her pretty pink bottom. "Do you trust me?"

"I do." She was breathing fast now and when he touched her, he found she was dripping wet. "Always."

He unfastened his breeches and stroked his shaft up against her flesh. She gasped again and then moaned. Holding on to her hips, he moved back and forth until she was panting. He pulled back just enough to ease into her pussy.

"Yes," he bit out. "God, yes."

He sank into her and she arched, her bottom flush against his lower belly. The next moment he began to thrust deep inside of her. She clutched the blanket in her fists as he rode her, her legs trembling as he held her up against him.

"Oh, my!" She writhed beneath him. "Yes!"

He pumped into her as she came, riding her as his own climax was imminent. With a shout he poured himself into her, holding tight to her as tremors shook his body.

Withdrawing after a few breathless moments, he righted her skirts and held her close in his arms. "Did you like that?"

Her eyes were soft. "I like everything we do."

He kissed her and held her for a while before they set upon their dessert picnic.

"Why have we never done that before, Will?" she asked after a while.

He could not help but grin. "Because every time we have been together, I am so eager to get inside of you."

"Hmm." She slid him a pretty smile of her own. "I

believe you must practice patience, husband."

He chuckled and they partook of their desserts as they basked in each other's company.

***

Brianna studied the beautiful man before her. Will was all hers, her wedded and beloved husband. She was so happy she could burst.

"What has you smiling so, wife?"

"This has been idyllic, Will. I shall cherish the memories of our honeymoon all of my life."

"Are you eager to return to Town, love?" he asked her.

"Hardly eager, husband. Though I am looking forward to living with you in your town house."

"Our town house." He winked. "And just think of it, you have never yet seen our bedchambers."

"Yes." She laughed lightly. "Only our parlor."

He gathered her to him and nuzzled her hair. "I cannot wait to live with you, Bree. In Town, here in Essex. Everywhere and for all time."

Her heart swelled and she wrapped her arms around his neck. "I do love you, Will."

"Forever?"

267

She nodded and kissed him. "Forever."

This was more than she could have wished for, her new life with him. She would do whatever was needed to keep her life and those that she loved safe.

They set off for London three days later, cuddling and kissing nearly all of the way. She had not been false when she had told him she would cherish the memories of their honeymoon all of her life. Once they returned to Town, there was the matter of John and his threats to consider. It was a great pity that she could not set it from her forever.

"We are at last home, love," Will said. "I regret to say that we only have two days before our ball."

"My sister would not like that you are expressing those particular feelings, Will."

"I am teasing, truly. It will be my absolute pleasure to celebrate our union with our friends." He arched a brow. "And more than a few acquaintances."

"If you prefer, we can host the ball at our town house."

He held up his hands in surrender. "No, no. Far be it for me to deny Lord and Lady Lacey of this honor."

She shook her head at him. "All right, Will."

They arrived back at the town house and alighted the carriage. Before she could take more than two steps he swept her into his arms and carried her up the steps past Carson, who held the door open with a barely subdued smile.

"Hello, Carson," Will said.

"Welcome home, Lady Shaston," he said with a bow.

She clutched Will's shoulders and bobbed her head at the butler. "Thank you, Carson."

Will laughed as he twirled her in the entryway before setting her back on her feet.

"Welcome home, dear wife," he said.

She took a breath. "Surely it was enough that you did so when we first arrived at Shaston Court."

"I only wish I had a third home to do so."

She clicked her tongue. "Really, Will."

"Will!" Violet came rushing down the staircase. "Brianna! You are back!"

"As you see, Vi," Will said.

Will's sister hugged Brianna tightly and then did so to her brother. "Did you enjoy your honeymoon?"

Brianna's cheeks flamed but she managed to hold her

countenance. "Yes, it was wonderful."

"And that is all we will say about it," Will put in.

Violet's eyes were bright. "And now you are back and there will be a ball two days hence."

"Dear, do let them catch their breaths," Will's mother said.

Will turned to her. "Hello, Mother."

He appeared surprised as she embraced him, but Brianna could see the love on the lady's face for her son.

"Hello, Lady Shaston," Brianna said.

"Nonsense, Brianna." She took Brianna's hands in hers. "You are my daughter now, so you may call me Mother if you like."

Brianna's throat grew thick. Her own mother had been gone since Brianna was very small and, while Aunt Hattie had admirably filled the void, this meant very much to her.

"Thank you," Brianna said. "Mother."

Will wore an expression of a cautious sort of happiness, but Violet's delight was clear.

"Mother says that after the ball we are to go back to Shaston Court."

"We must, Violet," Will's mother said. "William and Brianna deserve their privacy."

"Yes, yes." She tilted a look at her brother. "But next Season, Will? We can come and stay with you next Season, yes?"

"Of course, Vi." He placed a hand on her shoulder. "You both shall be very welcome."

Will's mother still appeared apprehensive about next Season but perhaps with time, and Violet's endless insistence, they would indeed both come to Town next year.

"I took the liberty of ringing for tea," Will's mother said.

"Thank you, that would be lovely," Brianna said.

They all turned to head into the parlor, Violet's happy chatter trailing behind the three of them. She stepped to join them when a floral arrangement caught her eye. There was a small bouquet of red roses on a table in the entry. Her heart stilled, and then tumbled to her belly.

"No," she breathed. "Please, no."

There was a card tucked within, addressed to her. It simply read, "One o'clock mews" with no signature. None was needed. Now her heart raced as she tucked the card deep into her reticule. Will could not learn of this. She would find a way to deal with John on her own.

"I cannot believe he requested a meeting in the wee hours again," she murmured.

Will turned back to her. "What is that, love?"

"Nothing, Will."

The lie left a sour taste in her mouth that she was certain would take several cups of tea to dispel. She took Will's arm and together they followed his family into the parlor.

Later that night, after Will had loved her most thoroughly in their very large bed, he slumbered easily beside her. She could not find sleep, however. How dare John send roses yet again? And to her new home with Will?

"Hateful man," she whispered, hugging herself.

She would not take money from Will. How ever would she convince John to leave her family alone? He wanted money, and she believed him when he had said he would not be denied. There was nothing else for it. He demanded to meet her again, but how would she put him off?

Marianne had not divulged all that John had done

to her back when it occurred. Brianna could still remember the stricken expression on her sister's face as she admitted all that had been going on two Seasons past. Marianne had been forced to be a courtesan to finance their Season in London, all for Brianna's society debut. Guilt bit at her anew, and tears slid down her cheeks.

The only thing that had prevented her from screaming at John there in the mews that night she had met him was that there was a nugget of truth in what he had said. Marcus and Marianne would never have found each other had circumstances not played out in the manner they had. Her beloved sister had been in more danger than Brianna could ever imagine, but for Marcus's love. Brianna would never forgive John for using Marianne so ill.

"Not as long as I draw breath," she grumbled.

Will stirred beside her. "Bree?"

She dashed her hands over her face and turned to him. "Here I am, Will."

He pulled her close, and she snuggled against his chest as his breath grew even again. She breathed him in, her face tucked against the base of his throat. There was a sublime comfort to be found in her husband's arms, and not only when he was sending her to the heavens with his skillful passions. She loved him and knew that he loved her.

The recognition of the fortune she had in him was finally enough to ease her toward sleep.

Chapter 16

In the morning, once Brianna had managed to get ready for the day after Will had awoken her in the most delicious manner, she made her way belowstairs. To her chagrin, the roses mocked her as she reached the entryway. She refrained from requesting that Carson dispose of them, reluctant to draw attention to the odious things. Instead, she held her gaze away from them as she turned swiftly toward the breakfast room.

"There is my lovely wife," Will teased. "Among the living once again."

Her face heated but she shook her head at him. "Good morning."

The rest of Will's family returned her greeting with their own as she served herself from the sideboard. She dropped a kiss on Will's cheek as she sat beside him.

"Are you ready for tomorrow evening's ball, Brianna?" Violet asked her.

"I believe so." She took a sip of tea. "Are you?"

"I am beyond ready, I daresay!" Violet said. "I cannot believe I get to attend."

"Why ever not?"

"I am not exactly out," Will's sister said.

"It is a party to celebrate your brother's nuptials, Vi," Will said. "You can attend without any sort of scandal following."

"Indeed, dear," Will's mother put in. "You may take all of the enjoyment in the party as possible, for it must last you until next Season."

The three of them chuckled as Violet pouted. "Yes, yes. I shall make do, I suppose."

"The time will fly, Vi," Will said. "It feels like only weeks since I fell in love with Brianna."

"It has only been weeks, Will," Brianna said.

He grinned. "And now you are well and truly mine, and no one can do anything to separate us," he said.

She smiled and set the horrid red roses from her mind. Will's heart was hers, and she would do nothing to betray it. Taking his money for John's blackmail was something she could never do. She had to speak to John, however. To somehow put him off until she could think of a solution that would not endanger her family. Or Will's! She was now connected to them and any scandal that touched Marianne and Marcus would touch them as well.

"Bree?"

She looked up to find Will looking at her, his brows raised. "Yes?"

He smiled. "You seemed miles away, love."

Shaking her head, she set her napkin down beside her plate. "I am sorry. Did you want something from me?"

"What say you to a ride in the park?"

"That would be lovely, yes."

They finished breakfast and readied for their drive. After donning her bonnet and gloves, she soon sat beside Will in his curricle like she had on that first morning he had officially begun to court her.

The summer morning was bright and clear, and the steady clop of the horses hooves helped her regain her mood and composure.

"This was just what I needed," she mused aloud.

"Why, in particular?"

"The sunshine, the outdoors." She nudged him with her shoulder. "The delightful company."

"Bree, I acknowledge that I endeavored to keep you in our bedchamber at Shaston Court, but we had ample outings in the fresh country air."

"That is very true." She sighed. "I suppose I simply wanted my new husband to myself again."

He pulled back on the reins and grumbled. "To yourself and about a hundred other souls this morning."

The path was quite crowded, and his carriage slowed to a crawl.

"Perhaps we should turn back," she said.

Will nodded and skillfully maneuvered the carriage off the path and onto a lesser trod track. "We should be home in just a few minutes." He laughed. "I am sorry you shall miss your great outdoors."

She clicked her tongue at him. Suddenly she caught sight of John standing beneath the trees just off the path. He stood in the shadows, but she could not miss his eyes that were trained on her. She stiffened, grasping on to Will's arm.

"What is it, Bree?"

He followed her gaze and saw John. To her astonishment, John dipped his head at Will as they passed him.

"What the devil is he doing here?" Will asked.

She held herself still. "Do you know him?"

"Not his name, no." Will craned his neck to watch John from his perch. "I have run into him several times this Season, however."

Bile rose in the back of her throat. Had John said anything to Will about her and her family? Of his demands?

"Where?" she choked out.

"At a public house." He shrugged. "At the boxing club."

"Did he…?" She cleared her throat. "Did he speak to you?"

"Yes, not that anything he said was of the friendly sort."

She took a breath to calm herself. "What did he say?"

"Nothing of any real import. He is a most distasteful fellow." His brow furrowed as he apparently recalled their interactions. "I will go to Joseph's and ask after him. Find out who he is."

"No!"

Will pulled the reins and stopped the carriage fully, turning to face her. "What is it, Bree?"

"Nothing."

"Nonsense. What is it about that man? Do you know him?"

She did not want to lie to Will, not so soon and not ever.

"Not really."

"Then you have seen him in Town as well?"

"I suppose I have."

"Did he speak to you?"

"Yes."

He gave a nod. "Then I did see him at the parties. I thought so."

"When did you see him, Will?"

"Before our wedding."

"He did not approach you, I daresay."

"No. I just caught sight of him on the fringes of the ballroom once or twice."

"Oh."

She was at a loss and could only pray that Will did not ask her any more pointed questions lest she be forced to tell him all of it.

"Strange gentleman," Will mused.

That was putting it mildly, in her opinion.

"Let us not speak of him, then."

"As you say, Bree." He placed his hand over hers and gave a gentle squeeze before taking up the reins again. "Why let him spoil our lovely morning?"

They continued on their way home from the park, the subject of John gone from their conversation but not from her mind. Perhaps she should speak with Marianne about this. No. She did not wish to upset her. Aunt Hattie, then. The woman kept her sister's secret all those weeks, after all. Surely, she would know how best to deal with John.

When they arrived home, the family took luncheon. She could scarcely attend to her meal, her mind swirling with all she had learned about John today. He had spoken to Will, and on more than one occasion? She longed to ask for the particulars, but she would not want to rouse Will's curiosity more than it apparently was. John's name was Filbrick, after all. Her husband was quite sharp and would soon link the man to her aunt.

"What say you to another picnic, Bree?" Will asked with a twinkle in his eye.

Brianna blushed at the knowing expression on his mother's face but thankfully Violet appeared oblivious to the implication.

"Oh, I have to go over some details about the party tomorrow evening," Brianna rushed out.

"I believe all is arranged," Will's mother said.

"Well, that is what I meant. I will pay a call on my aunt and check on the details."

"Do you want me to accompany you?" Will asked.

She waved a hand. "Oh no, Will. You will no doubt find these details more tedious than you did our wedding's."

He winced comically. "I believe I shall stay here and see to some work in my study."

They shared a sweet kiss, and she sought out Carson. She found the butler in the entry.

"Please call for the carriage, Carson? I shall be going to the Lacey town house."

"Very good, my lady."

She tapped her foot impatiently in the entry but was soon on her way to Marianne's. When she arrived, she asked for Aunt Hattie directly. Her aunt joined her in moments, wearing a sweet smile.

"Brianna, how lovely to see you." Her aunt embraced her. "I take it your honeymoon was all that you wished it to be?"

"Yes, Aunt." She looked about and did not see Marianne or Marcus at the moment. "I have to speak with you."

"What is it, dear?"

She shook her head. "Not here."

Her aunt nodded and they went into the library. Brianna shut the door and faced the other woman.

"Brianna, whatever is the matter?"

"John is in Town," she said without preamble.

"John?" Aunt Hattie's face paled. "No."

She nodded. "He is the one sending me the red roses."

Aunt Hattie appeared puzzled. "Why ever would he send you flowers?"

"To draw my attention." She took a breath and forged ahead. "He is attempting a blackmail."

She could see her aunt's mind working until finally she scowled. "Hateful boy. He is threatening to expose your sister."

Brianna was not surprised by her aunt's astuteness.

"Yes, and he is demanding money to keep his silence."

"I do not understand, Brianna. Millicent is wealthy."

"Millicent passed away and he received none of her money."

"Well, what of your uncle's bequest? John could not

have gone through all of that money so quickly."

"He claims he cannot touch his inheritance."

"That is passing strange. Your uncle had a fine head for business, if misplaced loyalties to his horrid son." She took Brianna's hands in hers. "You cannot pay him, Brianna. He would never stop coming for more."

"You know his character well, I daresay."

"He has none," she spat. "What he did to your sister? I could wring his neck even now."

"He will not stop, Aunt. I agree. And I learned today that he has approached Will on more than one occasion."

Her mouth dropped open. "Not about any of this?"

"No. I believe he was simply being his distasteful self."

Aunt Hattie cupped her cheek. "You are not to worry about this, Brianna."

"We cannot ignore this and hope that John ceases."

"Never mind. Let us focus our attentions on your wedding celebration. We shall worry about John after the party."

"It is tomorrow evening, after all," Brianna said.

"But John wants me to meet him at one o'clock in the morning, in the mews behind Will's town house. What shall I do?"

"You will not meet him, dear. That is certain."

Brianna blinked. "Do you mean, simply ignore his summons?"

Aunt Hattie drew her into her arms. "It will be all right, Brianna."

Brianna had no true notion that would be true, but she could only pray that it would be so.

***

Will stood in the Lacey ballroom, a grin fixed on his face. He could not dispel the expression, so pleased to be celebrating his marriage to Brianna with all of Society. He cared not that he might look to all and sundry like a besotted fool. He was in love with his wife and had no qualms about making that clear in company.

"Look at you, Shaston!" Lord Wilbrey joined him. "The very picture of the happy groom."

"I am indeed happy, Evan," Will said. "I could not imagine how happy marriage to Brianna would make me."

Evan placed his hand on Will's shoulder. "I am happy

for you, friend."

Will looked over the crowded room, easily finding Brianna. She stood with her aunt, and the two of them appeared to be in a close conversation. If he did not know her face so well, he could have missed the worry creasing her brow. It was gone in the next moment as she greeted another well-wisher.

"I must go see my bride, Evan."

"Go, please." His friend chuckled. "Lovesick swain."

Will made his way through the throng, accepting more good wishes as he went. He finally reached her and the delight on her face sent his worry flying.

"Will," she breathed.

He took her hand and kissed the back of it, as they were in company and her aunt was very close by. "Bree."

She wound her arm through his and sighed.

"Hello, Lord Shaston," her aunt said with a slight curtsey.

"Mrs. Filbrick, good evening."

"Are you enjoying the gathering?"

"I am, yes." He kissed Brianna's temple. "I love celebrating our marriage."

"As do I," Brianna said.

"Your marriage makes me very happy, Brianna," Mrs. Filbrick said.

There was a weight to the woman's words, though Will could not decipher her meaning at the moment.

"I am so very well pleased, Aunt," Brianna returned.

The older woman looked down at her own sleeve and tugged at the cuff. Will noticed a mark on her right wrist.

"Mrs. Filbrick, did you hurt yourself?"

"Yes, Lord Shaston." Brianna stiffened and her aunt nodded. "Nothing serious, however. Just a bit of a strain."

He looked from one woman to the other, seeing some sort of nonverbal communication pass between them. The older woman appeared concerned now, and Brianna gave a small shake of her head.

"Bree, is something troubling you?" he asked.

"No, Will." She cuddled closer. "I am a bit overwhelmed, I admit."

That was passing strange. He had never seen her anything less than poised in any social gathering, but perhaps as this party was in their honor she felt undue pressure.

"We are being celebrated, love." He stroked the hand grasping tightly to his arm. "Pray, be at ease."

"I am, Will. And so happy, truly."

Glancing at her aunt again, he caught something in her gaze but, before he could ask anything more, they were inundated with partygoers eager to give them their congratulations and best wishes.

Thankfully, they were able to escape the party well before it concluded. He was also grateful that his mother and sister had remained back at the Lacey townhouse, leaving them on their own at home.

"Did you truly enjoy yourself, Bree?" he asked in the carriage.

"I did, yes."

He truly wanted to inquire about her intense conversation with her aunt but, when she came closer and he caught her sweet scent, he set everything else aside. She was his wife. They were joined forever. And tonight, he would make love to her in their bedchamber as many times as he could manage before they collapsed together in a satisfied heap.

He readied for bed in his dressing room and when he emerged, clad in just his breeches, he found her pacing their bedchamber. Her thin nightgown swirled about her ankles but he forced his attention from her incredible figure to her worried expression.

"Bree?"

She stopped and whirled toward him. "Oh, Will."

Coming close, she wrapped herself around him. Her curves branded him, and he was instantly aroused. She trembled in his embrace, but he did not believe it was solely due to the closeness of her loving husband.

"Love, something is troubling you."

She gave a vigorous shake of her head. "Nothing is troubling me."

He gently grasped her chin and tilted her face up to his. "You can tell me anything, Bree."

Her gaze searched his before she looked away. "There is nothing to tell."

"I do not believe you, but I know your heart. This must be something very troubling for you to keep it from me."

"I want to tell you, Will." She nibbled her lower lip, and then her expression crumbled. "I am afraid I cannot," she sobbed.

"Shh, love." He urged her over to the bed and they sat beside one another. "You kept my secret, Bree." He wound his fingers with hers. "You may depend upon me keeping yours."

"That is the crux of the matter, Will." She sniffled and faced him again. "It is not my secret to keep."

Chapter 17

Bree stroked the back of Will's hand, hoping against hope that he would not press her further.

"It is related to your family," he said. It was clearly not a question.

She nodded.

"You can tell me anything, you know."

"It concerns something that occurred two Seasons past, Will."

His brow furrowed but then her very clever husband appeared to put things together. "Lacey and your sister."

Her heart clenched. "Pray, tell me you have not heard anything untoward about them."

"No, love. I have heard no tales carried."

Relief swamped her. "Marcus made Marianne's acquaintance some time before he began courting her."

He tilted her a look. "I believe he was courting you, Bree."

"That was trivial, believe me. He was besotted with my sister, and I could not be happier with how matters resolved themselves."

This brought a soft smile to his face. "I can only agree

with you, as we are now together."

"But looked at in a certain light, their previous involement might be construed as…unseemly."

"Unseemly?"

She covered her face with her hands. "She was his courtesan," she whispered.

Will's silence was deafening. "Ah."

Lifting her head, she studied him. "Are you certain you knew nothing of this?"

"I had heard whispers that Lacey was enamored of his particular lady, Bree. I am certain there must have been a very good reason they were together in such a manner. Your sister is not a light o' love."

"There was a reason, Will. My detestable cousin John Filbrick, Aunt Hattie's stepson, forced Marianne, leaving no other avenue open to her."

He paled. "I know full well how it is to feel powerless. Please know that I do not judge your sister."

"Oh, Will." She wrapped her arms around him. "You are the most noble of men."

He rubbed her back again and for several moments she relished the comfort.

"Did Lacey know of it, Bree? At the time, that is?"

"He did not. His money essentially paid for my Season, though I did not know it at the time."

"No one else knew of it?"

"I believe Lord Devlin may have known. I have caught snippets of his conversations with Marcus that might indicate that he helped both the earl and my sister."

"Devlin is a good man."

Bree nodded. "His wife Penelope is very happy."

Will appeared thoughtful once again. "Your family had no money to speak of?"

She shook her head. "My uncle passed away, leaving everything to John and nothing to my aunt."

"Or to you and your sister."

"That is correct. I am still certain the dear man had other plans, but I suppose legally John was the only heir."

"And your cousin did nothing to provide for you?" Will cursed. "Scoundrel."

"He is that."

"But what, pray, does that have to do with your current upset?"

She took a breath to steel herself. "John is attempting a

blackmail."

"He is looking to blackmail Lacey?" His brows rose. "Is he mad? The man will see him dead before letting scandal touch his wife."

"No, not Marcus." She paused a beat. "Me."

"What?" Will stood, his hands fisted at his sides. "I will kill him with my bare hands."

She grabbed on to his arm. "No, Will. You cannot approach him."

"Why the bloody hell not?"

"He will spill his story, and my sister and Marcus will be ruined."

He raked his fingers through his hair. "What, pray, do you wish me to do then?"

"Nothing. I have spoken with him, and I believe I can put him off."

"You met with the scoundrel? When?"

"Before we wed."

He studied her and then his manner shifted. "Ah, love." He touched her face. "Is this the reason you tried to cry off?"

"Yes. Please know that I never had any doubts

about marrying you."

"I do know that now. But it is wonderful to hear it."

She smiled at his obvious love for her.

"But Bree," he went on, "how did he contact you?"

She swallowed. "He is the one who has been sending the red roses."

Will cursed loud and long. "Where did you meet him?"

"In the mews behind Marcus's town house."

"Was it just the one time?" he asked.

"I only met with him once, but my aunt met with him last night."

"Your aunt met with him?"

She nodded. "Behind our town house."

"Why would she risk such a thing?"

"She feels responsible for all of it, Will."

"How could she be?"

"I agree the blame all lies with John, but I could not dissuade her."

He glanced down at his hands and then back up at her. "Her wrist, Bree. He hurt her."

She sniffled again. "It appears so."

"That could have been you." He held her close again.

"And now knowing what a piece of filth he is, it could have been so much worse."

"There is more, Will. He wants me to take your money to pay him."

"I would gladly pay him if I thought for one moment that would be the end of it."

They settled on the edge of the bed again, and she was grateful for the support. Her relief nearly made her swoon. "I am so glad I finally told you of it."

"You can tell me anything, Bree. I do not understand one thing, however. If he received all the money from your uncle, why is he in such dire need of funds?"

"He said that his wife left him nothing when she passed."

"That still does not explain his financial situation, especially if he inherited everything from your uncle."

"He claims that he cannot access the money he inherited."

Will's expression sobered as he clearly puzzled through it all.

"There is something more to this, love. More than

he is admitting." He wrapped his arm around her. "We will get to the bottom of this." Straightening, he looked at her with wide eyes. "Bree, what does he look like?"

"He has dark hair and would be considered pleasant looking if one did not know of his nature. He is very strongly built as well."

"Strongly built? I believe he is the he gentleman that I have seen now and again. The one we glimpsed in the park yesterday."

She blew out a breath. "Yes, the man in the park was John."

"He is a most distasteful person. The first time I saw him in the pub, he put his hand on one of the serving women. And now, to hear all that he had done to your sister and was attempting to do to you now?"

Will's face showed his anger anew.

"Promise me, Will?" She framed his face with her hands. "Promise me that you will not seek him out?"

He stared deep into her eyes and her breath held. Finally, he nodded with obvious reluctance. "All right, but I would sorely like to pound my fist into his face for what he did. Not just to your sister, as abhorrent as that is. But to threaten you?

To put his hand on your aunt? It is beyond the pale."

"Aside from everything he has done, I would not be able to bear it if anything happened to you."

"I will keep my word and not go looking for trouble, love." He kissed her tenderly. "Your family is mine now, Bree. And I will keep their secrets as well as you have all these years."

She could not resist throwing her arms around his neck. "Oh, Will."

He held her closer still, stroking her hair as she trembled in his arms. Soon she could not help but feel the tension leave her as longing filled her. He was hers, this marvelous man, and she would make love to him with all of herself.

She kissed him, and he soon returned the embrace with growing vigor.

"I love you, Bree." He trailed kisses over her throat. "I would die if anything happened to you."

His words, his loving, caused her heart to soar. Her body was not far behind as he bared her breasts and began to worship her flesh. She was nearly lost in sensations as one of his hands moved to her center. She was achy and hot, a flush tripping over her body as he roused her.

"You want me, Bree." He dropped a kiss on her belly. "Tell me you want me."

"I want you, Will." She moaned and opened her thighs for him. "Please."

When he settled between her legs, it took precious little to send her to the heavens. She cried out as her orgasm hit, and he came up and kissed her.

"You liked that, love," he said, stating the obvious.

"Oh, yes." She opened her eyes to find him grinning down at her. "You look quite pleased with yourself as well."

He shook his head. "Not yet."

She pushed at his shoulder, and he rolled onto his back. "Then let me ease you now."

Kissing him, she trailing her fingers over his taut belly until she found him. He was hard and ready and she could not wait to get him inside of her.

"You want me, Will," she said, turning his words on him. "Tell me you want me."

He groaned and nodded. "Christ, yes I want you."

She came up on her knees and straddled him. "You are

ready for me."

"Please, Bree."

She shifted and slid down on him, taking in all of him. He held tight to her hips as she began to ride him, driving both of them toward bliss. Her body began to quiver as his movements became wilder. He arched, closing his eyes as he sought climax for both of them. He was beautiful, her husband. And strong and noble. She was so lucky to have him all to herself. That was her last coherent thought until she came apart.

As if from far away, she heard him shout her name as he followed her. She collapsed on him, breathing in his fresh scent as she snuggled against his chest. His heart hammered in her ear, and she could not help but smile.

"You enjoyed that," she sighed.

"I enjoyed you, wife." He withdrew from her and took a deep breath, still holding her close. "Mmm."

He sounded drowsy so she pulled the coverlet over the two of them and cuddled closer.

"Good night, Will."

He yawned. "Good night, love."

Though she was tired, and so thoroughly satisfied, sleep was elusive. Will had promised not to seek out John, but what if her cousin decided to contact him?

She squeezed her eyes shut and prayed that would never happen.

***

Will sat at his club the next afternoon, eyeing every gentleman as they entered. He had never seen Brianna's cousin John Filbrick here, but he would not put anything past him.

He and Brianna had seen his mother and sister off to Shaston Court this morning, and he was vastly relieved that he would not have to worry about their learning of all that Brianna had divulged last evening.

Brianna's revelations still shocked him now. He held no ill will toward Lacey or his wife, for he had seen firsthand how much they loved each other. He would never do anything to expose them or hurt Brianna's family in any way. How dare the scoundrel approach her!

"Shaston, you appear quite fierce," Lord Wilbrey said as he joined him.

"Hmm?" Will shook his head. "Forgive me, Evan. I was

simply ruminating on a matter."

"What matter, pray?"

"I cannot speak of it. It is of a delicate nature, and not my tale to tell."

"That piques my interest tenfold, but I will not press you."

They sat in silence before a gentleman caught Will's eye. He straightened and lifted his hand in greeting.

"Ho, Devlin," he called.

Lord Devlin, a dark-haired gentleman of their circle, smiled and approached their table. "Hello, Shaston. Wilbrey."

"Hello, Devlin," Evan returned.

"Sit, pray," Will said.

"Thank you, I shall." Devlin sat and grinned at Will. "As I saw that you were all but overrun during your party at Lacey's, let me once again give you my felicitations on your marriage, Shaston."

"I am the luckiest of men," Will said.

"As I too consider myself so, I am most pleased for you and Miss Brianna."

Evan rolled his eyes. "Please, do not press upon me the merits of a happy marriage."

"Ah, Evan," Will said. "When you inevitably fall, I predict it will be a sight."

Devlin chuckled. "He is woefully misinformed, Shaston."

"I believe so, yes."

"My Penelope is my heart, and I am not ashamed to admit it," Devlin said.

"Well said, Devlin," Will said.

"You have but to look to your sister and brother-in-law for evidence, I wager," Devlin said.

Will froze. Marcus and Marianne Lacey were at the crux of his wife's dilemma at present. Brianna had told him that Devlin had been of some great service to Lacey two Seasons past. He could not ask about that particular subject in company, however.

"That is a very dark look, Shaston," Devlin said.

"What?" Will blinked. "Pardon, I am in a conundrum."

"One he would not share with me at present," Evan said.

Will looked from one gentleman to the other before leaning toward Devlin. "May I ask something of you,

Devlin?"

"Certainly."

"Do you have the means to do some investigation?"

"Why ever would you believe that I would…" Devlin's face took on a shrewd expression. "You know," he said in a low voice.

Will slowly nodded.

"Know what, pray?" Evan cut in.

He and Devlin each held up a hand to quiet him. Evan huffed and crossed his arms, but he did not press either of them for more information.

Devlin thought for a moment and then nodded. "My solicitor has been known to get to the bottom of matters for me in the past. On more than one occasion."

"This is intriguing." Evan sat up straight. "Do you have salacious gossip, Devlin?"

Devlin frowned at him. "I do not."

Will heard the chill in his voice, as well as the steel. If this man did indeed keep Lacey's secret, then he was the one to advise Will on his next move.

"This does not concern any gossip, I assure you,"

Will said. "I would very much like to have the name of your solicitor, however."

"You shall have it, of course." Devlin studied him. "And pray, let me know if I may be of any assistance."

Will dipped his head in thanks. "I shall."

Evan let out a low whistle, causing Will and Devlin to stare at him.

"If I am to be kept out of this little intrigue, let us at least play a hand or two of cards," Evan said.

"Capital idea," Will said.

They spent the better part of an hour in pleasant occupation and, before Devlin took his leave of the club, he wrote down the name of his solicitor.

"You will find Grimes to be quite sharp, Shaston." He leveled him a look. "And the man is the very soul of discretion."

"Thank you, Devlin."

"My offer stands."

Will nodded and Devlin left. He dealt the cards for a two-handed game and could feel the curiosity burning in Evan. It was not long before his friend spoke.

"I must broach the subject of this investigation, Will."

Will shook his head. "I cannot say anything, Evan. Do not take this personally, pray."

Evan's lips thinned. "You have divulged certain matters before, so I have to assume this does not have anything to do with you in particular."

Will raised his brows. His friend was quite astute when he wished to show it.

"It does not, but that is all I will say at present."

Evan held his hands up. "I trust you to tell me when you can. I will not pry further."

Will smiled. "You are a good friend, Evan."

Upon arriving back home later that afternoon, Will wasted no time in contacting Lord Devlin's solicitor. Hopefully Mr. Grimes was available to meet with him in much haste. Surely Devlin's man would be able to help find something to take the teeth out of John Filbrick's threats.

After instructing Carson to see it delivered directly, he settled back at his desk. Leaning back, he gazed out the window toward the gardens but did not really see them. He could not push the pressing matter from his mind.

It took everything within him to keep from seeking out Filbrick himself, but he had given Brianna his word. How dare that reprobate endeavor to put Brianna in such a position! Now knowing what he put Lady Lacey through, it should come as no surprise.

"Bloody bastard," he bit out.

"Will?"

He turned to find Brianna standing in the door to his study. Fierce protectiveness seized him, and he stood and crossed to her. Wrapping her in his arms, he let out a heavy breath.

"Ah, love."

"What is it, Will?" she asked softly.

He leaned away slightly, keeping his arms around her. "I promise you and your family will stay safe."

She tilted her head. "I know you do, and I believe you."

He kissed her and held her close, praying that he would be able to keep his promise.

Chapter 18

Brianna attempted to hold her countenance as the party seemed to go on without her. She was present, though her mind was too often engaged with the subject of John and his distasteful blackmail scheme. It had been a relief to speak of it all with Will but, while he had promised not to approach John, she knew how furious he was about the entire matter. He was a very good man, her husband.

"Why do you look troubled, Brianna?" Patrice gasped. "Oh, do not tell me that certain aspects of married life have proven...overwhelming?"

"What?" Brianna glanced over at her friend as her question penetrated. Laughter bubbled up. "No, Patrice. Not overwhelming in the least."

Patrice appeared to mull over Brianna's words before slowly nodding. "I have seen the heated looks between my sister and Lord Devlin, Brianna. When they seem to believe they are the only two persons in the room."

Brianna's cheeks flushed hot. "It is astounding when such regard exists between husband and wife."

Patrice shivered. "I am afraid to give all of myself in that manner."

"I can assure you that is a great blessing, Patrice. To share that kind of love and regard."

"And that is what you and Lord Shaston share?"

She could not keep her smile hidden. "Very much so."

Her friend shook her head. "I shall not fall victim to such feelings, I daresay."

Brianna leveled her a look. "Oh, my dear. You most certainly will, and there is no telling when."

"As you say."

Brianna could not argue with her at this point in time. Patrice had not yet fallen for her particular hero, and no amount of encouragement would lead to a match when the girl was not ready.

"I shall yield to you, Patrice. Although you may want to reconsider your determination in the matter."

Patrice made another maidenly protest, but Brianna did not attend her. No, she had caught a glimpse of a dark-haired gentleman out on the terrace. A shiver coursed down her spine. *John.*

"No." She gasped. "It cannot be."

"What is the matter, Brianna?" Patrice grasped her arm. "Truly, you have gone quite pale."

Brianna could not voice an answer, for her heart was pounding and her throat tight. Oh, where was Will? If he saw John, she could guess full well what he would do.

"Come." Patrice gently tugged her toward the terrace. "Let us get a breath of air."

Brianna's feet were stuck to the floor. "No, not the terrace."

"All right." Patrice looked about. "The refreshment table, then. A glass of lemonade may be just the thing."

Brianna searched the crowd for any sign of Will. She had to be certain he was not heading for the terrace.

"Lord Shaston!" Patrice called.

Brianna froze and then relief crashed over her. Will was heading in their direction.

"What is it?" Will asked.

"Brianna appeared faint just now, Lord Shaston," Patrice rushed out. "We were talking about, well never mind what we were talking about, when she seemed to freeze."

"Bree, love." He took her chilled hands in his warm ones. "What is the matter?"

She gazed into his beautiful blue eyes and began to come back to herself. "Will."

He smiled, though he had not lost his worried expression. "Yes. Are you all right?"

She managed to give a nod. "Yes."

He stroked the back of her hand with his fingers, calming her. "That is a relief to hear."

Patrice handed him a glass of lemonade and he thanked her. "Drink this, Bree."

She took a sip of the sweet drink and began to ease. "I have something to tell you, Will."

"What is it?"

She could not say anything here, in the crush of partygoers at the refreshment table. Will seemed to grasp the situation and turned to Patrice.

"Miss Patrice, may I bother you to search out Lord Wilbrey?"

Patrice nodded and left them.

He led Brianna toward the potted plants set in one alcove. "Can you tell me now?"

"I believe John is here."

Will's cheeks reddened. "Blackguard," he growled. "Where?"

"The terrace." He began to take a step when she grabbed onto his jacket sleeve. "No, Will. You cannot approach him. You promised me."

He cursed softly and raked his fingers through his hair. "As you wish, Bree."

Lord Wilbrey and Patrice soon joined them.

"Here I am, Shaston. At your service."

"Wilbrey, I need you to go out onto the terrace. There is a certain gentleman out there."

"The prickly gentleman, I presume."

Brianna blinked. Did Lord Wilbrey know of John as well?

"Yes," Will went on. "Pray, speak with him and find out what he is doing here. I highly doubt he was invited."

He and Lord Wilbrey exchanged a look of some import, though Brianna could not guess the meaning. Wilbrey left, and Will leaned closer to Brianna.

"That gentleman does not know Lord Wilbrey,

Bree. He will not connect us."

"But Lord Wilbrey seemed to know of him, Will."

"Only from our conversations. He has never set eyes on him, and the blackguard will not recognize him either."

"I pray you are right."

"What is going on?" Patrice asked.

"We cannot speak of it, Miss Patrice. Please forgive our odd behavior."

"Odd? Yes." She smiled. "Intriguing, most definitely."

Will blinked at her but Brianna at last found a smile.

"You have no part in this, Patrice," she said with a touch of her hand on hers. "Count yourself fortunate."

Patrice held up her chin. "I can keep secrets, you know."

Both Brianna and Will gaped at her.

"Secrets?" Brianna whispered.

Patrice waved a hand. "I do not possess any at the moment, but I can be the sole of discretion."

Brianna doubted that very much, but she would not say so. She had always known her friend to be an open book. This was not the time for frivolity, however.

"Yes, I am sure," Brianna said.

Lord Wilbrey returned not ten minutes later. He

appeared puzzled and quite put out.

"That man is no gentleman," he grumbled.

"What did he say?" Will asked.

The blond gentleman looked toward Patrice and then leaned closer. "He puffed up and said that he was more than welcome at such parties, or at least he would be very soon."

"That is passing strange," Patrice said.

"He was indeed lurking, searching for someone I assume."

Brianna's stomach churned. "Oh?"

"He did not divulge whom, however." Lord Wilbrey appeared embarrassed. "He had some ungentlemanly things to say about the ladies present."

"Brianna and myself?" Patrice asked.

"No, dear Miss Patrice. Just the ladies he happened to see out on the terrace." He shook his head. "I would not repeat the things he said."

"Scoundrel," Will spat.

"Indeed," Lord Wilbrey's eyes narrowed. "Is this regarding the matter you were discussing at the club?"

More silent communication between the two men

followed this until Will nodded.

"Yes, I am afraid so."

"I will not press you for information," Lord Wilbrey said.

"Thank you," Brianna said to him. "You are a good friend."

The man splayed a hand on his chest and dipped his head. "I am honored, Lady Shaston."

Brianna smiled at Will's particular friend, grateful that he did not seem put out by their lack of shared information. John had the temerity to come to a Society function without an invitation? He was as brazen as he was disgraceful.

"Are you ready to depart, Bree?" Will asked softly.

She looked into his beloved face and nodded. "Yes, pray."

They made their farewells and returned to their townhouse. Cuddled against Will in the carriage was a balm to her heart, which was a very good thing.

Even so, she had serious doubts that she would be able to sleep at all tonight.

***

Two days later, Will sat in the office of Lord Devlin's

solicitor. The gentleman had written directly after Will's request, which was no great surprise as Devlin relied on him so heavily.

Mr. Grimes was a capable, neat-looking man with dark hair and spectacles. His office appeared well-managed and tidy as well. Will felt a touch of relief as he took note of all of this.

"I thank you again for meeting with me, Mr. Grimes."

"Certainly, my lord. Lord Devlin wrote that this was a matter of some delicacy."

"Indeed, yes. It involves my wife's family." He swallowed his disgust. "And a man named John Filbrick."

"John Filbrick, you say?" Mr. Grimes asked. Will nodded.

"That name is familiar," the solicitor said as he turned to look through his files. "Let me see."

Will studied the man again. Will did not know the whole of the man's assistance to Lord Devlin, but if he trusted him Will would do likewise.

"John Filbrick is a relative of the Earl of Lacey's

wife," Grimes said. "Her cousin."

"Yes, and my wife's cousin as well."

Grimes raised his brows. "You married Miss Brianna Ellsworth?"

Will could not keep the smile from his face. "I did, yes."

Grimes appeared thoughtful for a moment, and then let out a breath. "I trust I may share what I learned about the lady two Seasons past?"

"About Brianna?"

"About all the ladies Lord Lacey was considering that Season."

Will nodded. "I shall hold it close."

"Miss Brianna and her sister, now Lady Lacey, were on the earl's short list of possible brides. There was an issue with their finances, however."

"And, if I recall, that mattered not in the least to Lord Lacey."

Grimes gave a small smile. "Indeed. It seems that the young ladies were orphaned when they were quite young, which I am certain you know."

Will nodded.

"They were then taken in by their aunt and her husband,"

Grimes went on. "When that gentleman passed away, he left his estate to his only child. His son from his first marriage, that is. The aunt and the ladies received nothing."

Will knew full well about this occurrence, and it caused his anger to surge anew.

"But what about John Filbrick? If he inherited the estate and money, why is he…?" He leaned forward. "Filbrick claims that he has no access to his inheritance. Can that be possible?"

"I cannot imagine why that should be. But now about John Filbrick, there is little said of him that is good in their part of Shropshire."

"Did you speak to him yourself?"

"Yes. I went to the man's place of residence and spoke to him. He had kind words for his stepmother, though they rang a bit false."

"What of the Marianne and Brianna?"

"He spoke fondly of Miss Brianna but his comments regarding Miss Marianne… I suppose I would call his manner boastful."

Will could well imagine why but did not wish to

speak of it.

"What other impressions did you have?" he asked.

Grimes shifted in his seat. "Well, he told me that he gave the ladies enough money to set themselves up in Town for the Season. Said that was more than should be expected of him, after they had lived off his father's largesse for most of their lives."

From the distasteful contact Will had with the man himself, he did not find the solicitor's words hard to believe.

"I have spoken to him myself and he is a blackguard to be sure." Will swallowed. "And I believe I know why he would appear boastful."

Grimes nodded. "He smiled in what I would call an oily manner and said he was amply rewarded for his generosity and considers any debt repaid."

Will knew full well to what Filbrick had been referring, and disgust swirled in his belly. How dare he boast about what he had done to Brianna's sister?

"What, precisely, do you need me to find out for you, Lord Shaston?"

"I need to know of the whole of the man's financial situation, Grimes. As I said, he claims he cannot access his inheritance. I believe you should start there."

"Anything else?"

Will thought about all that Brianna had told him. "He also asserts that he received nothing from his wife's passing."

"Nothing?" Grimes shook his head. "Perhaps that lady was quite smart where it came to her husband."

"It does explain why he is so desperate for money, if one did not consider his father's bequest. He has been bothering Brianna nearly since the beginning of this Season."

"How does this involve Lady Shaston?"

"He has been threatening my wife. Blackmailing her."

Grimes appeared shocked. "How so?"

"He wants her to steal from me to pay him what he believes he is owed." Will paused. "To keep quiet about Lady Lacey and their family."

"Quiet about what, pray?"

Will took a breath. "The manner in which Lord Lacey first made his wife's acquaintance."

Grimes narrowed his eyes. "He is a scoundrel, to

be sure. I am glad you came to Lord Devlin and to me, Lord Shaston."

"What can you learn?"

"I believe we need to take away his ammunition, but I take it this information cannot be divulged to the *ton*?"

"No, it must not ever be known. There must be another way."

"Let me investigate his finances and see precisely why he cannot access his father's money. It is passing strange."

Will nodded. "That will be a good place to start, I believe."

"Do you truly believe he can be put off until we get to the bottom of the matter?"

"I am hopeful, Grimes."

"I do not believe him to be an honorable man in any sense of the word, Lord Shaston."

Will came to his feet. "If he so much as thinks to approach my wife again, it will not go well for him."

Grimes stood as well and held out his hand. "I would not wish to be in the man's boots."

"Nor I." Will shook the man's hand. "Thank you, Grimes."

Grimes nodded and Will returned to his carriage. He prayed that the solicitor would find something to use against Filbrick.

Otherwise, Will would have to take matters into his own hands.

Chapter 19

Brianna sat in the parlor of Marianne's townhouse two days later. She sorely needed the respite from the constant worry over John and his threats, and the chance to see her loving sister would hopefully be the balm she craved.

"Bree!" Her sister breezed into the parlor, a wide smile on her face. "I am so glad you were able to join me for tea."

"I was surprised by the invitation," Brianna said.

"Why?" Marianne's eyes sparkled. "I know, I know. I have not been very social of late."

"Oh, but you have Marcus and little Hannah to keep you occupied."

"That is very true." Marianne rang for tea and sat beside her on the settee. "I do miss going to the parties with you, Bree."

"I do not believe you have missed very much."

Marianne blinked. "But you always so enjoyed the parties."

Brianna shrugged. "I prefer staying home with my husband."

"You and I are of a like mind." The tea cart arrived, and Marianne poured each of them a cup. "Though I had hoped you could share some of the news of the *ton*."

Brianna laughed. "You were never one to trade in gossip."

"I shall keep secret anything you tell me. Thus, I am not trading."

"A clever dodge." Brianna took a sip of her tea and set the cup back down. "I know this is a difficult subject, but have you heard from John at all this Season?"

"John?" Her sister paled and pulled back. "Our hateful cousin?"

Brianna nodded.

"No." Marianne gave a shiver. "I never want to hear from that horrid man again."

Relief washed over Brianna. "That is good to hear."

Marianne stood and crossed to the doors. She looked about and then pulled the door shut. Brianna watched as she warily returned to the settee.

"Why ever would you ask about John, Bree?"

Brianna could not tell her about John's threats or his repeated efforts to meet. Marianne had built a wonderful life with a man who loved her. She deserved to continue in happiness, she and Marcus and their sweet baby girl.

"I was just thinking about when we came to Town two years ago."

A shadow crossed Marianne's gaze. "That was a dark time, the beginning of the Season."

"I know." Brianna covered her sister's hand with hers. "I cannot thank you enough for what you did for us."

"I only did what was needed, Bree. For you and for Aunt Hattie."

Tears pricked Brianna's eyes. "I am so pleased that your life turned out so well."

Marianne nodded. "I am happier than I ever imagined I could be. Even before John."

Resolve steeled Brianna's spine. "That is wonderful to hear."

"Where is our dear aunt this afternoon?" Brianna asked after a bit.

"She is out making her own calls."

Brianna recalled how happy their aunt often appeared at the parties, sitting with her acquaintances among the ladies of a certain age.

"I am glad that she has found her own circle."

"She deserves her happiness, after Uncle left her with nothing."

Brianna shook her head. "Uncle was mad about her, Marianne. How could he not make provisions for her?"

"Or for us?"

"Not necessarily, although I am certain that our aunt would have taken care of us."

"She did, Bree. She does."

Warmth spread through Brianna's chest. "Yes, she does."

She thought of the threats John made toward all of them, and that warmth was replaced with hot anger. She could not show such to Marianne, however. Her sister was quite astute and would pick up on any change in her demeanor.

"Now," Marianne said, brightening. "Do tell me if Patrice Prestwick has encouraged any suitors thus far this Season?"

Brianna found a smile, ever grateful for the diversion. "I do not believe so, sister."

"Why not? She is as pretty as her sister Penelope, after all."

"As are all of the Prestwick sisters," Brianna added.

"They are the most pleasant girls, all of them." Marianne's brow furrowed. "I would think that Miss Patrice would be eager to get out of the Prestwick house, however. I believe it can be quite…noisy."

Brianna nodded as she thought back to a visit she paid there at the very beginning of the Season. Like most of the times she had been at the Prestwick house, the sisters had chatted and laughed throughout the afternoon. Penelope had been absent, no doubt ensconced with her Lord Devlin, but the three remaining ladies had adequately filled her absence in the parlor.

"Yes, I would agree that Patrice should wish to quit the house."

"And set up her own, perhaps?"

"I have not seen any marked attention on her behalf." Brianna thought for a moment of their conversations at the party the other night. "Although…"

"Although?"

"She and Lord Wilbrey seemed to enjoy each other's

company when we were all talking together."

"Hmm." Marianne nibbled on a biscuit. "Perhaps it was the subject at hand."

"What do you mean?"

"What were you all discussing?"

Brianna froze. They had been speaking of John for the most part, though Patrice and Lord Wilbrey did not know the whole of it.

"Nothing of import, truly," she finally answered.

"Then perhaps Patrice finds Lord Wilbrey's polished good looks very much to her liking."

"He is handsome, Marianne."

"Indeed, he is." Her sister nodded. "And very gallant."

Brianna could see the wheels spinning in her sister's head and could not help but grin. "I have never known you to matchmake, sister."

"I suppose it is the fate of all happily married ladies to help other ladies enter into the same condition."

"Are you saying that next Season I may endeavor to do likewise?"

Marianne arched a brow. "Are you not hosting

Lord Shaston's sister then?"

Brianna was flummoxed. "I had not thought of that."

"You and your dear husband shall escort her to the parties next Season, little sister."

"And we shall pass judgment on all of her potential suitors?"

"Naturally."

Brianna's shoulders slumped. "I do not believe I am ready for that."

"You will be, Bree." Marianne winked. "You will be."

"How?"

"Consider matters from this perspective. You will only have one young lady to lead."

Brianna caught her sister's meaning. "Oh, poor Aunt Hattie."

The two of them fell to laughing as they recalled all of the headaches they had innocently brought upon their aunt during that Season. So many suitors had swarmed around her and her sister, though Marianne drew much more notice than Brianna without even attempting it. Except for Marcus, that was. Little did he know at the time that he was already in love with her!

An hour or so later, she was back in Will's carriage and headed for home. All of what her sister had said, and not said, echoed through her mind. Marianne was deservedly happy, and that was after all that she had gone through.

Brianna would do whatever was necessary to make certain that John never touched Marianne's life again.

***

Will smiled at Brianna as dinner was served in their dining room. The evening was to be just the two of them, and he could not be happier about the prospect.

"I am most pleased that you suggested foregoing the parties this evening, Bree."

She nodded absently, and he caught the worry etched on her brow.

"Is everything all right, love?"

She shrugged in answer, so he turned his attention to his meal of pheasant and vegetables. As he ate, he took note of how little she did so. She pushed her food around the plate, taking the occasional nibble or two.

"Truly, Bree. You are clearly troubled."

She placed her fork beside her plate and sighed. "I

admit it, Will. I am."

"About what, pray?"

When she did not answer right away, instead eyeing the servants serving at table, he cast a meaningful look in Carson's direction. The butler waved the servants out of the room and closed the doors, leaving them in privacy.

"Bree, you can tell me anything."

"I know that."

"Then what is troubling you? Did you not enjoy your visit to your sister's this afternoon?"

"I did, yes." She stifled a sob, but he caught it. "She has a wonderful life, Will. Hard-earned and everything that she truly deserves."

"Yes," he acknowledged.

"Nothing can be allowed to harm it. To take it away from them!"

"Easy, love." He had not yet told her of his enlisting Grimes to get to the bottom of matters, but perhaps it was time. "Bree, I have something to tell you."

"What is it?"

"With the help of Lord Devlin, I have engaged a solicitor to untangle the matters of your detestable cousin."

"Oh, Will!" Her eyes rounded. "Tell me you have not spoken of all that occurred two Seasons past?"

"Not all of it, love. I enlisted him to ferret out the truth of John Filbrick's financial situation so that we can have all the ammunition we might need."

"We might need to do what?"

"To force him to abandon this blackmail scheme and leave you in peace."

"You promised me that you would not approach him, Will."

"And I will not." He swallowed. "Until I have proof of his true situation."

She crumpled her napkin and twisted it in her hands. "I suppose we must."

"We?"

"You will not do this on your own." She squared her shoulders and met his gaze directly. "I must be able to secure my sister's, and my family's, futures."

Pride joined the love filling his chest. "You have my word that I shall share this with you, Bree."

She took a breath and then nodded. "Thank you, Will."

"Now, eat your dinner," he ordered with a smile.

Laughing lightly, she took up her fork again and ate with a bit more enthusiasm.

Afterward, they retired to the parlor.

"A game of cards, Bree?"

"Patience, Will."

"The game?" He arched a brow. "Or are you advising me to bide my time?"

She patted the seat next to her on the very comfortable settee where they had first been together.

"The game, I think."

He grumbled playfully. "As my wife wishes."

She took the deck of cards from a small drawer in a side table, which he then carried over in front of the settee. He settled beside her again and drew her closer.

"Are you quite certain, love?" he asked.

"Indulge me, Will."

He kissed the side of her neck. "Always."

She giggled and began to place the cards on the table. The game of solitaire was not often played by two, but they took turns flipping the cards and discarding them. He took every opportunity to stroke her hand or her thigh as they both began to breathe a little faster.

When her fingers trailed over his hand and up his arm, he nearly trembled. She always had this effect on him, and he could not be more grateful that she appeared to be just as affected as he was. She was flushed and lovely, and he could not keep from touching her.

"Will," she sighed.

He brought his face to her throat and breathed in her sweet scent. "Yes, love?"

"You are driving me to distraction."

He nibbled on her earlobe, earning a gasp of delight. "That is fully my intention."

She turned to face him, dropping the cards on the table. She cupped his face with both of her hands. "You are my favorite distraction, Will."

He kissed her, taking what she offered when she opened her mouth to him. Her taste flooded his senses, sweet and pure. His tongue swept through her mouth as he pulled her closer to him.

"Ah, Bree."

She wound her arms around him now, her fingers driving through his hair.

"Damn, I have on far too many clothes." He pulled at his cravat and unbuttoned his collar. "As do you, love."

She nodded and pushed his jacket from his shoulders. "It seems as though we should do something about that."

He shed his jacket and eased the bodice of her dress down until the tops of her breasts were begging for his kisses. Burying his face in her cleavage, he breathed her in. When he began to drop kisses on her silken skin, she sighed and leaned her head back.

"Mmm, yes."

Lifting her skirt, he trailed his fingers over her leg until he found her center. She gasped with delight as he began to stroke her.

"Do you want me, Bree?"

"Of course, Will." He touched her more fully and she trembled in his arms. "Oh, my."

He was so intent on pleasing her that he did not realize her clever hands had worked the buttons of his breeches free until she grasped him. He groaned and thrust toward her touch.

"Do you want me, Will?" she countered on a whisper close to his ear.

"Damn, yes," he managed to say.

Grabbing her hand, he placed it on his shoulder as he urged her onto his lap.

"I cannot wait, love," he rushed out.

She laughed and then moaned as he spread her thighs with his. He moved his fingers in and out of her until she was panting for release.

"Please, Will."

He shifted and readied her for him. "I shall try my best, Bree."

In one motion, he lifted her hips and pulled her down on him. She cried out, so close to her climax. He was not to be far behind, he knew.

She clutched at his shoulders as they moved together in rhythm, climbing higher and higher until she peaked. Sobbing, she leaned back wearing her pleasure on her beautiful face.

Finally, he closed his eyes and drove higher still, coming deep and high inside of her. She collapsed against him, and he held her close.

"I love you, Bree," he rasped.

She murmured something in agreement and buried

her face against the base of his throat.

After several moments reveling in their bliss, Will moved her off of him and they rearranged themselves. She cuddled close as he looked about the parlor. Cards were scattered on the floor and the table was askew.

"I daresay our card game is over," he quipped.

"Perhaps." She kissed his neck. "But this was far more pleasurable."

"I agree wholeheartedly."

A knock came at the door, and they separated a bit more.

"Come," he called.

Carson entered, a worried expression on his face. "A missive has arrived, Lord Shaston."

Will stood and crossed to the butler. "At this time of night, Carson?"

"It appears so, my lord."

Will took and opened it, quickly scanning the contents. He absently took note of Carson's leaving them in privacy once again.

"What is it, Will?" Brianna asked.

He shook his head and read it through again. "It is from Devlin's solicitor."

She stood and joined him, grasping his wrist. "What does he say?"

"It seems that your cousin lied, Bree."

"About what, pray?"

He handed her the letter. "About everything."

She scanned the words Grimes had written, shock clear on her face.

"He denied Aunt Hattie her inheritance?"

"And you and your sister of yours, love."

"We all have inheritances?"

"Yes. You are each quite wealthy."

"Truly?"

"Your aunt's share of your uncle's estate is twenty thousand pounds."

"Oh!"

"And you and your sister each were meant to have fifteen thousand pounds."

Tears filled her eyes. "I knew our uncle was a good man who would provide for us."

The man had to be a damned sight better than his wastrel son.

"I wish I had known him."

"What does all this mean, Will?"

"It means that Filbrick is very desperate that this information never come to light. His father left him very little in comparison."

"That would explain his anger, I suppose. Can he truly not access our money, then?"

Will shook his head. "He cannot."

"That is good." She sniffled. "Blackguard."

He wrapped her in his arms, stroking her back. "This settles it, then."

"What?"

"We must speak to Marcus and your sister."

She pulled back, her face pale. Then she nodded.

"As you say."

He cupped her cheek and kissed her tenderly. "It will be all right, Bree."

She nodded, and he prayed he was right.

Chapter 20

Brianna wrung her hands in the carriage as they rode the short distance to the Lacey townhouse. Will placed his hand over hers to still them. His touch was warm, and it managed to go a little way toward calming her.

"Take a breath, Bree. We will talk to them together."

"Must we, Will?" She took in a shuddering breath. "I would do anything to spare my sister from this."

"They deserve to know what is going on, love. Lacey is reasonable."

"Usually, yes." Brianna shook her head. "But with this situation with John? I can well imagine his ire when he hears that his family is being threatened."

"True. But we now have a path forward. We have a way to take the wind out of Filbrick's sails, so to speak."

"His sails." She fisted her hands now. "I would scuttle his boat, if I got the chance."

"Scuttle?" Will's brows rose. "My dear wife knows about sailing?"

She shrugged. "Not truly, though I have read about

it in novels."

"Hmm." He placed an arm around her shoulders. "You shall have to share these novels with me, I think."

"Why?"

"I cannot worry that you will be charmed away by a seagoing gentleman one of these days."

She dropped a kiss on one corner of his smiling mouth. "I know what you are about, husband."

"You do?"

"Do not play the innocent." She picked up one of his hands and placed a kiss on the back of it. "I know you are trying your best to distract me."

He gave her a crooked smile. "Did it work?"

"A bit, yes. Thank you."

"I take it you did not mention anything about this coming conversation in your note to your sister this morning?"

"No." She sighed. "I hope she is not worrying over this."

"I do, as well."

The carriage rocked to a stop, and they alighted. Will appeared resigned and oh so very committed to their course. Taking her cue from him, she squared her shoulders and rapped sharply on the front door.

Marianne herself pulled it open. "Bree!"

She reached out and grabbed Brianna's wrist, tugging her into the house.

"Marianne!"

"Shh," her sister said. "Hello, Lord Shaston."

Will followed swiftly and shut the door. "Lady Lacey."

"Marcus is waiting for us in his study," Marianne whispered.

They followed her down the hall to the study. Marcus stood within, a brooding expression on his face.

"Quickly," Marianne said, all but pushing her and Will into the room.

Once the door was closed tight Marianne let out a breath. "There."

"Where is Aunt Hattie?" Brianna asked.

"She is abovestairs."

Brianna and Will exchanged a look.

"What is going on, Shaston?" Marcus cut in.

"This is sensitive, Lacey." Will ran a hand over his hair. "There has been a development of which you and Lady Lacey should be made aware."

"Then, sit." Marcus sat behind his desk and leaned forward. "Tell me everything you know."

Brianna took Marianne's hands in hers and tugged her toward the settee set to one side in the room while Will sat across from Marcus.

"This is a sensitive matter, Marianne," Brianna said.

"Is this about whatever was troubling you yesterday?" Marianne asked. "About John?"

"Yes." Brianna took a breath. "About everything, actually."

Her sister appeared very nervous until she caught her husband's eye. Marcus gave her a look full of warm affection and compassion, and she visibly calmed.

Marcus faced Will again, and his eyes narrowed. Then he nodded. "You have been working with Grimes."

"Devlin told you?" Will asked.

"He did, yes. He did not tell me the nature of your query with the solicitor, however."

Will looked at Brianna, and she read the question in his gaze. She gave him a nod and he looked toward Marcus again.

"This is in regard to John Filbrick, Lacey."

"Marianne's cousin?" Marcus cursed low and long. "If I

ever see that man, I shall happily wring his neck."

"He is in Town," Will said.

Marcus surged to his feet. "Where?"

"Marcus, please," Marianne soothed.

"What is going on, Shaston?" Marcus growled.

"He has attempted a blackmail."

"He approached you?"

"Yes, but not in this matter. I have had a few run-ins with him, though I did not know his identity at the time."

"He is blackmailing me," Brianna said in a small voice.

Both Marianne and Marcus began to pepper her with questions about the whens and wherefores, but Will held up a hand to still them.

"He has pressed her to take my money," Will said. "He claims that he does not have money to live on."

"He has been in contact with you, Bree?" Marianne asked.

Brianna knew there was nothing else for it. "He has been sending me the red roses, Marianne."

"What?" Marcus asked.

"And he has approached me on more than one occasion," Brianna said.

"Here is yet another reason for me to kill the bastard," Marcus said.

"I received information from Grimes late last evening," Will cut in, saving her from divulging more of the hateful things John had said about Marianne and their family.

"And?" Marcus asked.

"It seems that he was truthful when he told Brianna that he received none of his late wife's inheritance."

"Millicent died?" Marianne asked.

"Yes, several months ago. Grimes could find no hint of foul play, but the woman had done her best to tie her money and holdings so Filbrick could not touch anything."

"Smart woman," Marianne allowed.

"There is more," Will went on.

"He lied, Lacey. About Mrs. Filbrick and our wives."

"What about us?" Marianne asked.

"Your uncle left your aunt, and the two of you, substantial inheritances. Inheritances totaling fifty thousand pounds, actually."

"Fifty…" Marianne sucked in a breath. "How did he

conceal such a sum?"

"Poorly, as it turns out," Will said. "Grimes has already set in motion the required documentation and procedures to see the money settled on the three of you."

"Aunt Hattie was left twenty thousand pounds, Marianne," Brianna said. "And you and I, each fifteen thousand."

Marianne let out a little sob. "That means that had I known, I would not have had to do all that I did two Seasons ago."

Marcus stood and Brianna moved to allow him space to comfort her sister.

"Now, love. Just think of it." He grasped her chin and lifted her face to his. "Even if you had been independently wealthy, I would still have fallen for you."

Marianne sniffled and Marcus cradled her in his arms.

"I am sorry for all that you went through, Marianne," Brianna said. "I know it was horrid but now we know the truth."

"And Filbrick has no more leverage over any of

you," Will said.

"He will be even more desperate, Shaston," Marcus faced Will again. "Something must be done about him."

"I wrote Grimes back this morning. He is compiling a list of his transgressions," Will said.

"No!" Marianne shouted. "No one must know of what John did to me. Of, of, of what I did afterwards."

"Pray, do not trouble yourself," Will rushed out. "No mention of you or what you went through will ever be made public."

Marianne's relief was palpable, and when Marcus stood, Brianna took her hands.

"All will be well, Marianne," she said. "You have our word."

Marcus held his hand out to Will. "I cannot thank you enough, Shaston."

"Do not thank me yet. There is still the matter of ending his scheme."

"How do you intend to do so?" Marcus asked.

Will appeared thoughtful. "Let us both think on it, Lacey. Between the two of us, we shall find a way to make certain the bastard never harms either of our wives ever again."

***

Will sat in his study that evening, once again reading over the letter from Grimes. He knew the man would see to the financials of the ladies, but at the moment he was more concerned with gathering proof of the bastard John Filbrick's crimes. And the man still thought to blackmail Brianna?

"Never."

A knock on the opened door drew him. He found Brianna standing there. Worry was etched on her beautiful face.

"Bree, what is it?"

She shook her head and held out a note. He stood and crossed to her, and then took it.

"It is from John," she said.

Anger surged through him as he read through the foul man's words. Alarm soon made his anger flee as he reached the end of the short message.

"He demands to meet you tomorrow evening?" he roared.

Brianna placed a hand on his chest. "Easy, Will."

"You will not meet with him."

Her eyes were downcast. "I must."

"No." He shook his head. "I will not allow that man to get anywhere near you."

"We have to put an end to this."

"Letting him get close to you again is not the way."

"This cannot continue, Will."

He took her hands and tugged her closer. "I know, love."

She turned and cuddled against him, and a fierce protectiveness washed over him. His mind worked over possible solutions to their predicament.

"I think I know of a way to catch Filbrick in his lies, Bree."

She lifted her head, and he could see the hope bloom in her expression. "How?"

"Lacey and I will go to meet him."

She shook her head. "He would never meet with you."

"Regrettably true. A man who would threaten you and your aunt is a coward at heart."

"I shall meet him."

"No, love."

"Not alone, Will." She touched his face. "You and

Marcus will be nearby."

The thought of her with John Filbrick, even with himself close by, was enough to chill his blood.

"I cannot let you dare such a thing."

"He will not hurt me with the two of you nearby."

"You do not know that. He is getting desperate, love. From all that Mr. Grimes said, Filbrick's money is all but gone. There is no telling what he would attempt."

"I trust you to keep me safe."

He gaped at her. "You do?"

She met his gaze evenly. "I have a very devoted husband, after all."

"You do, love. But the thought of putting you in such a position frightens me to my core."

"Then we must make certain that everything goes well."

He eyed her expression now, and it was full of determination. "You are very brave."

Her eyes sparkled. "I am."

"And daring."

A small smile played over her lips. "Yes."

He blew out a breath. "All right." He sat behind his

desk again and took out a sheet of foolscap. "I shall write Lacey and advise him of our coming battle tomorrow."

She winced as she sat across from him. "Perhaps do not refer to it as a battle?"

He caught her eye and managed to smile himself. "You have the right of it. I saw the murder in his eyes when your cousin's mere name was mentioned."

He penned a note to Lacey regarding their plan to have Brianna meet with John, with them secreted close enough to keep her safe.

"I will request that Mr. Grimes join us," he said. "He can hear everything your cousin divulges and, with the evidence he has already discovered, there will be little chance of the blackguard getting away with anything."

"You are very clever, husband."

He lifted his head to find her wearing an expression of self-satisfaction. He clicked his tongue.

"Do not appear so self-satisfied, wife. I realize that you are flattering me because I bent to your wishes."

She grinned at him. "Perhaps."

"Do you think we should bring your aunt into this?"

Her eyes rounded. "Oh no, Will. I would not wish to

worry her."

"It involves her inheritance, Bree. As well as her dear departed husband's true wishes."

"Yes, and we will share all of the information with her once John is well and truly vanquished."

"Vanquished? A bit bloodthirsty, are you?"

"I am. He hurt Marianne. He has terrorized me and dared to put a hand on my aunt."

"I agree wholeheartedly, which is another reason I wish to have Mr. Grimes there."

She blinked, and then nodded sagely. "Marcus will be less likely to strangle John if the solicitor is there."

"Precisely."

Chapter 21

Brianna suppressed a shiver as she settled into the carriage beside Will. They rode together with both Marcus and the solicitor toward the meeting location John had indicated. Marcus wore a scowl and Will seemed quite apprehensive. As for Mr. Grimes, the neat-looking solicitor, he appeared to have a touch of excitement for their adventure this evening. His eyes were bright behind his spectacles, even as his expression remained mostly sober.

"Are you all right, Bree?" Will asked, taking her hand in his.

She patted his arm. "I could ask the same of you."

"I am concerned about your well-being, love."

"As am I." Marcus cleared his throat. "I daresay your sister would never forgive me should that bastard—forgive me, Brianna—should Filbrick so much as touch you."

"With all good luck, this should put an end to all of Mr. Filbrick's schemes," Mr. Grimes said.

"From your lips to God's ears," Will said. "Thank you again for the suggestion of making use of your carriage tonight."

"I reasoned that it would not be recognized should Mr.

Filbrick look about before meeting with Lady Shaston," Mr. Grimes said.

"Sound notion, Grimes," Marcus said.

Will nodded in agreement and peered out the window beside him. "It is of no surprise that the man selected a pub for their meeting."

"Not in the pub precisely, Will," Brianna said.

"True. He is far more careful than that," Will growled.

"Devious, one might say," Marcus added.

Brianna tamped down her own apprehension just as the carriage came to a stop.

"I instructed the driver to park at a fair distance, Lord Shaston," Mr. Grimes said.

Will and Marcus nodded, and then they both turned looks of concern in her direction.

"Do not look at me so, pray," she said. "You are making me quite nervous."

"We will be within earshot, Brianna," Marcus said.

Will took her hands again. "And I shall not take my gaze from you, love."

The three gentlemen alighted, and then Will held

her hand as she stepped down. She drew the hood of her dark cloak over her head and took a breath. The air was tinged with salt and damp, and the smell was not pleasant. The cobblestones beneath her shoes felt slippery, and she carefully made her way toward the alley. John had instructed that they meet outside of the pub, which appeared to do a good business tonight, and for that she was grateful.

As she arrived at the appointed location, she turned to make certain that she could not see Will or the other gentlemen from her vantage point. The carriage was shrouded in a welcome spot of darkness, and she knew that they secreted themselves nearby.

Taking a breath, she steeled herself for the coming confrontation. She reminded herself that John had no way of knowing that they had unraveled his scheme. He was coming from a position of perceived power, and that would have to keep her safe. Until she divulged what they had learned, that was.

She shifted and her right foot brushed against something on the ground. Considering the neighborhood, she was almost afraid to look down. The clouds shifted and gave enough light to see that it was a red rose. She nearly snorted. Her cousin was far too predictable. Instead of the fear that he no doubt had intended the token to rouse, she was seized with renewed determination. This would end now.

"My dear cousin," he drawled from the darkness just beyond the patch of moonlight.

"John."

"Did you manage to get me the money, Brianna?"

"Why, precisely, do you need the money?"

She could feel his irritation and, when he stepped closer, she saw his scowl.

"I told you. Millicent tied up her money so that I have nothing," he grumbled. "I lay the blame at her father's feet. The man never liked me."

Wise man. "You have money from our uncle, John. Why do you not make use of it?"

"Do not dare to tell me how to handle my finances."

"But you have not handled your finances very well up until now, have you?"

He came closer still. "I will have the money I need, dear cousin. From your very wealthy husband. Or perhaps from your sister's."

"They will not give you anything."

"That is unfortunate."

"I may have the money to give you myself, it turns out."

"What?"

"Yes, it seems that you were not entirely truthful when our uncle died."

His eyes rounded. "What are you saying? I gave you enough to come to Town, did I not?"

"You hurt Marianne, John. Do not attempt to rewrite the past by saying that you gave her anything out of the goodness of your heart."

"She snagged herself a very wealthy earl, Brianna. True, she snared him on her back, but don't most proper young ladies do likewise?"

Her stomach churned with disgust. "Do not speak of it."

"Sweet, innocent Brianna. Do not pretend that you did not find your own very enviable position the same way?"

She slapped him. "Stop talking so."

He rubbed his face and, in a fast motion, grabbed her wrist. "Attempt that again, little cousin, and I shall make you very sorry that you have led me on a merry chase these past months."

Alarm coursed through her. He had forced Marianne, had he not? Was Will close enough to prevent such from happening to her should their plan go awry?

"I am sorry," she bit out. "Take your hand from me."

He ran a haughty gaze over her and finally removed his hand from her. "Do not goad me to show you more of my ire."

"What did my uncle truly leave you, John?"

"What do you mean?" He paled slightly. "He gave me all that he had."

She clicked her tongue and shook her head. "Liar."

Fear flickered over his shadowed features. Fear and a good dose of guilt.

"You know nothing, little cousin."

"I know that he was a good man and provided for his beloved wife."

"He did not!"

"He did. And for Marianne and myself, as well."

He grabbed her again, by her arms so that she was pinned in his hold. "What do you know?"

"I know that you are destitute for one very good

reason."

He brought his face close to hers. "And what is that?"

"You cannot access the money that was left to the three of us."

"It is my money," he spat. "I deserved it, not that woman and you two. It took some doing, but I made it seem as though he left you nothing."

"How?"

He appeared quite proud now. "I falsified his will, Brianna."

"Then what we were told was a lie?"

"Indeed. It was as if he left you nothing, which he should have. Perhaps he would have done so, had he known how poorly you would all turn out."

"Uncle loved us, John."

"I was his son!"

"Yes, and perhaps he knew full well just what type of man you had become."

"I deserve that money!" He shook her until her teeth rattled. "I want the money he left you. And since I cannot access it, I will have your husband's money."

"I am not giving you any money."

He looked as though he would strike her, but then he lifted his chin. "I shall tell all and sundry just how your sister met her husband. How she took lovers until she snagged the prize of the Season."

It was a good thing he still held her arms for she would have slapped him again for his hateful words. God knew what he would have done to her had she done so.

"And your own beloved husband would learn how your family comported themselves two Seasons past. No doubt he would leave you in a thrice, lest the unseemly scandal touch his family."

She had no such fear. Will loved her, and he would never leave her. They kept each other's secrets safe. John did not know she had that faith, however. Truly, he had no notion of such devotion.

"What did you do to Marianne, John?"

He laughed, an ugly sound. "I bought her virtue, Brianna. By paying for the three of you to escape to London, I earned every bit of her delectable body."

Revulsion nearly made her vomit. She only hoped that Marcus could withstand the filth John was spewing at the moment.

"She said you forced her."

"She lies. I may have been rough with her, but that only served to prepare her for her new livelihood, didn't it?"

"You forced her," she insisted.

John muttered something under his breath. "All right, I forced her. She grew timid when the time came to give me my due, so I took it."

"Did Millicent know?"

"Millicent did not know a thing."

"She must have suspected your true character, seeing that she left you no money."

"She and her father betrayed me, as my own father did."

"You deserved precisely what you got, John. Nothing."

He slammed her against the wall behind her, sending the breath from her body.

"You will give me your husband's money!"

"I will not."

"I will tell all about Marianne. Perhaps I shall embellish the tale to include you and your aunt in the enterprise."

She was stunned speechless.

"Quiet now, dear cousin? You are as beautiful as your

sister, I daresay. Now that your husband has no doubt taught you how to please a man."

She read the lustful intent on his face and squeezed her eyes shut. He came closer, his breath coming fast. In the next moment, he was pulled from her and thrown against the wall himself.

"Keep your filthy hands off of my wife," Will growled.

She was grateful for the wall at her back, for her knees nearly buckled beneath her. It was as if all of the bravado she had summoned for this encounter fled her in a rush.

***

Will was beside her in an instant, cradling her close as she buried her face against his chest. His heart was still pounding as he breathed her in. The stench of the waterfront faded in the wake of her fresh, floral scent.

"You are all right, love." He kissed the top of her head. "You are safe."

"Oh, Will."

As if from afar, he heard Marcus threatening John

to keep still as Mr. Grimes repeated everything John had admitted to her. Will glanced over and watched as John appeared to sink into himself. It was not with shame, he would wager. He sincerely doubted that the man was capable of such an emotion. It was fear that his actions had finally been laid bare for all to see.

"You committed fraud, Mr. Filbrick," Mr. Grimes said. "I have uncovered the true will and confirmed that the three ladies were indeed provided for."

"Those miserable women are lying, and…" John's tirade ended with a choking sound.

"Watch your tongue," Marcus said.

"And you committed an assault on an innocent young woman as well," Mr. Grimes continued, undeterred by John's attempted slander.

"He nearly did so to Brianna," Will added, his fear returning in a rush. "Thank God he did not."

"Have you summoned the Watch, Grimes?" Marcus asked.

"I have indeed, Lord Lacey."

"Lacey, do you and Grimes have things in hand?" Will asked, his eyes on Brianna once more.

"Yes, Shaston. See to Brianna."

Will lifted her chin and studied her face. She was pale but did not seem to have any injuries. "He did not hurt you?"

She shook her head.

"Thank God for that as well," he said.

He held her close to his side as they returned to the carriage. Once inside, he embraced her. "My brave, daring Bree."

"I was so scared, Will," she admitted on a whisper.

"One would never have guessed it from how well you held your own with that bloody bastard."

"What he said about Marianne. About my aunt and me." She trembled. "He is the very worst of men."

"Grimes and the Watch will see that he pays for everything that he did."

"He will not be able to approach us again, will he?"

"Never." He rubbed his hands over her back. "Never, ever again shall you be put in such danger."

She smiled at him now, her eyes shining with tears. "You kept me safe, Will."

"And I would do so again." He hugged her again, unable to keep from touching her. "Pray, do not get yourself into another such predicament, love?"

"I shall try."

He frowned at her, and then laughed. She began to giggle, and it was as if a rush of relief crashed over both of them there in the solicitor's carriage.

When Lacey and Grimes joined them nearly twenty minutes later, Will had managed to regain his composure.

"I take it Filbrick is taken care of?" he asked Grimes.

"The bastard will be going to prison, Shaston," Lacey said.

"Where he shall remain for some time."

"Then, there is a possibility that he will be out some day?" Brianna asked.

Grimes shook his head. "He is both friendless and penniless, Lady Shaston. And from what I have seen of his demeanor, he shall only make enemies there."

"We shall keep track of him, love," Will said. "Will we not, Grimes?"

"Indeed."

"I cannot wait to get home and tell Marianne that it is all

over," Lacey said.

"It is over," Brianna sighed. "Thank you. All of you."

"Nothing like this will ever touch you again, Bree." Will kissed her cheek. "Never again."

Will could not shake his unease even when he had Brianna safe and sound at home. His hands trembled as he readied for bed, and he gave them a shake before clenching them tight.

"She is safe," he whispered to himself.

When he emerged from his dressing room, he found her cozily tucked into their bed. Her hair was down and her smile was sweet as he joined her.

"I am so grateful that this is all behind us, Will."

He stretched out beside her and held her close. "I could have killed him when he grabbed you."

"If he had not held my arms at my sides, I would have done."

That startled a laugh out of him, surprisingly.

"You are the most daring woman I have ever known."

"I would dare anything to keep my family safe."

She kissed him and stroked his face. "And to keep your secrets, too."

"You are everything to me, Bree." He shook his head. "Speaking of everything, I have a question for you."

"Yes?"

"Now that you have your inheritance, what can I possibly give you?"

She shrugged one shoulder. "Love."

He grinned and held her close. He had thought that his secrets were his own to guard. That he only had to feel ashamed of his weakness. Then Brianna knocked on his door late one night and the Season would never be the same.

She had shown him that he was a good man and that he was worthy of her love. She protected her family and drew him into the circle of that affection. Even his mother and sister had been affected by her giving heart.

He had her and she had him, and nothing would ever dare to touch her again.

Epilogue

Brianna sat at Shaston Court, working on her correspondence. There were already starting to receive invitations for the coming Season, and it would take some juggling to keep them all straight.

They would soon go to Town, and she suspected that this Season would prove to be a challenge to be sure. Will's little sister Violet would accompany them for her first time out in Society, and Brianna suspected that they would have to be ever vigilant to keep her from getting herself into trouble. She grew tired when she even gave thought to all it would entail.

"Are you still at your desk, Bree?"

She looked up to find her very handsome husband grinning at her. "We are proving quite popular this year, Will."

"I believe it is due to the air of mystery."

"Mystery?"

"Yes, love. We went to very few parties after silencing your despicable cousin."

"I know, but I did not want to catch wind of any gossip due to John's horrid scheme."

"From what Wilbrey has told me, no tales were spread about your family. Besides, your cousin has no friends in Society."

"That is very true."

"As much as I loved spending the winter here at Shaston, I admit I am looking forward to the coming Season."

She slanted him a look. "Do you forget we will have a charge this year?"

Will waved a hand. "Vi shall be little trouble." He barked out a laugh. "Even I do not believe that."

She set the papers and quill aside and stood. "We shall persevere."

He pulled her into his arms, and she reveled in the warmth of his embrace. His warm and spicy scent struck her, and she breathed him in.

"I am nearly exhausted just thinking about the round of parties we shall have to attend," she admitted.

"You?" He kissed the top of her head. "My daring wife?"

"I am no wallflower, that is true." She knew she must tell him the truth of it now. "I just know I may be a bit fatigued some evenings."

"Fatigued?" He pulled back to study her face. "Why ever should you be, save for my every effort to keep you in our bed."

She laughed and shook her head. "I have a confession to make."

He arched a brow. "Do tell."

"It seems that Hannah will soon have a little cousin."

He stared at her for a long moment and her heart raced. Would he think it was it too soon to have a child? Oh, she prayed it was not so.

"A baby." He took an audible breath. "A baby?"

The most beautiful smile spread across his beloved face, and he hugged her to him. "A baby! Ah, this is remarkable!"

"Not so remarkable." She laughed. "Not when one considers just how often you keep me in our bed."

He laughed as well and held her close. "We are a family now, Bree. And if our child is half as daring as its mother, they shall keep me very busy indeed."

"Oh, I hope not then."

"Why?"

"I want to keep my husband busy with me."

He stroked her cheek. "But you are well, love?"

She nodded. "Yes. The doctor paid a call just yesterday afternoon."

"Where was I?"

"I believe you were out on the estate."

"Hmm. Clever of you."

She grinned.

He kissed her and cupped her face. "I love you, Bree. Always."

"And I love you, Will. You are quite stuck with me."

"Happily."

She knew she was blessed to have such a man. One who would save her from herself, if need be. He might consider her the daring one, but he was just as brave.

She was the luckiest woman in England.

About the Author

JoMarie DeGioia is a bestselling author of Historical and Contemporary Romance. She's known Mickey Mouse from the "inside," has been a copyeditor for her tiny town's newspaper, and a bookseller. She is the author of over 50 published Romances and writes Young Adult Fantasy/Adventure stories and Paranormal Romance too. She gets lost in DIY projects around the house and discusses plot ideas with her dogs and cats. She divides her time between Central Florida and New England.

Discover other books by JoMarie DeGioia

The Secret Hearts series including

The Courtesan Countess

The Charming Champion

The Daring Debutante

The Bridgewater Brides series, including

The Heir's Treasure

The Viscount's Vixen

The Earl's Beauty

The Gentlemen Undercover series, including

A Hero and a Gentleman

A Hero and a Rogue

Shopgirls of Bond Street series, including

That Determined Mister Latham

The Dashing Nobles series, including

More Than Passion

Pride and Fire

Just Perfect

More Than Charming

The Cloud Canyon series, including

Chasing Dreams

Secret Dreams

Wildest Dreams

The Cypress Corners series, including

Finding Harmony

Taming Jake

Loving Cassie

Winning Ben

Showing Jessie

Seeing Shannon

Dreaming Eli

Giving Chase

Kissing Bree

Wishing Joy

Bugging Nate

The Gifted Young Adult Fantasy/Adventure series, including

Gifted

The Braunachs of the Dell series, including

Luke's Gold

Patrick's Promise

Sexy Historical Novellas, including

In the Lady's Heart

In the Baron's Bed

In the Knight's Chamber

Connect with me online

Get the latest news!

Be a VIP Reader!

Twitter: https://twitter.com/JoMarieDeGioia

Facebook:
https://www.facebook.com/JoMarie.DeGioia.Author

Website: www.jomariedegioia.com

Made in the USA
Middletown, DE
03 September 2024

60291297R00222